# CURE FOR
# WEREDUCK

**Dave Atkinson**

NIMBUS
PUBLISHING

# Young readers' praise for WEREDUCK

I rate *Wereduck* 10/10 and will be one of the first to buy the next books.

—*John*

I really enjoyed reading your book! You are an amazing author and I hope that I will become one too.

—*Bonnie*

I'm writing to thank you for coming all this way to our West Royalty Elementary School and telling us about *Wereduck*. I loved it. I read it all. It's AMAZING! Good luck in your new book. I hope it's as good as *Wereduck*. I wasn't into reading too much but when I read your book I loved it so now I'm reading more!

—*Diego*

Nimbus Publishing Limited
3731 Mackintosh St, Halifax, NS B3K 5A5
(902) 455-4286 nimbus.ca

Printed and bound in Canada

NB1212

Cover and interior illustration and design: Jenn Embree

This is a work of fiction. Names, characters, incidents, and places, including organizations and institutions, are either the product of the author's imagination or are used fictitiously.

Library and Archives Canada Cataloguing in Publication

Atkinson, Dave, 1978-, author
Cure for Wereduck / Dave Atkinson.
Issued in print and electronic formats.
ISBN 978-1-77108-445-1 (paperback).—ISBN 978-1-77108-446-8 (html)
I. Title.

PS8601.T5528C87 2016          jC813'.6          C2016-903732-0
                                                 C2016-903733-9

Nimbus Publishing acknowledges the financial support for its publishing activities from the Government of Canada through the Canada Book Fund (CBF) and the Canada Council for the Arts, and from the Province of Nova Scotia. We are pleased to work in partnership with the Province of Nova Scotia to develop and promote our creative industries for the benefit of all Nova Scotians.

*To the duck I met that time in Stratford, with apologies.*

# PROLOGUE

LAURA WOKE UP WITH A GASP. THE ROOM WAS DARK.

She stared at the ceiling, the sound of her pulse pounding in her ears. She drew deep breaths to calm her racing heart.

Her hand fumbled on the night table for her glasses. She put them on and looked at the clock. It was 2:34 A.M.

Laura swung her legs over the side of her bed and padded on bare feet to the top of the stairs. She descended to the kitchen. The glow from the clock on the microwave lit her way to the sink. She poured herself a glass of cold water and carried it to the back door.

*Calm down,* she told herself as she peered through the screen. *There's nothing out there. There's nothing to be afraid of.*

She knew it was a lie. There was something to be afraid of. She'd known for fifteen years. Everyone told her it was her imagination, but her nightmares were as real as the glass in her hand.

She knew from experience she wouldn't get back to sleep tonight. She could return to her bed and watch every minute of every hour creep by. Or she could turn on her computer and lose a couple of games of chess to anonymous people on the internet. Or she could—

She gasped. That sound.

*Howling.*

Her glass fell, shattering into a thousand tiny pieces. It was her nightmare, but real.

"No," she blurted. Her head shook back and forth, willing the sound from her ears. "No, no, no...."

She was losing control, and she could feel it. Her fear was taking over again.

*Get a grip, Laura,* she told herself. *Get control. Get....*

Her eyes grew wide.

She strode to the living room and flicked on the lamp by the couch. She approached the bookshelf and pulled down a cigar box from the top shelf. She blew dust from the lid.

*Get control,* she thought. *Take control.*

Laura closed her eyes. She forced herself to listen: a chorus of howls, just as she'd feared.

*No*, she thought, straining to hear. *Not quite.*

It wasn't the low, terrifying howl she'd heard in her dreams. It was higher, more frantic. This was something else.

"Coyotes," she said aloud. "It's just coyotes."

She had read somewhere that coyotes were moving into this part of the country. She had just never heard them *here* before.

She carried the box to the kitchen and placed it on the table. She turned to the calendar on the wall and searched for the familiar and ancient symbols most people overlooked.

"The full moon isn't for a few weeks," she whispered to herself. "Of course. It's just coyotes."

She collapsed into a chair, laying her cheek on the cold surface of the table. She breathed in and out, counting to four between each breath until she calmed down.

She sat up and pulled the box toward her. She traced its edges and corners before she flipped open the lid and reached inside. Her fingers wrapped around familiar, cold steel as she drew out the revolver.

She had always hated guns. In her earlier life, she would never have imagined the amount of time she would spend researching and reading through gun catalogues before selecting this very one. More specifically, for the single bullet that sat loaded in its chamber.

It turns out they don't sell silver bullets at your neighbourhood gun shop.

# CHAPTER ONE

KATE STOOD FROZEN ON THE THRESHOLD OF THE small, wood-framed house. Sunlight streamed around her body, showing the dark-haired girl in silhouette. She held a knapsack in one hand and a pillow in the other.

"Um, Aunt Bea—" began Kate. She stared into the living room, eyes wide. "Bea?"

Bea strode up behind her with suitcases in her hands. She peered around Kate into the house. "What is it? What's wrong?"

Kate and her family were tired from a long journey. They had driven two days without rest from New Brunswick to southern Ontario, moving all their worldly possessions—few as they were—to Aunt Bea's house. Until this moment, the only thing on thirteen-year-old Kate's mind was the thought of a soft bed to crash on.

"You never told us," said Kate, slowly pronouncing each word, "that you have a cat."

A grey tabby stirred in the corner of the room. It sat on a couch cushion and began to wash its paws.

"*Cat*?" came a voice. "Did somebody say *cat*?"

Kate's eleven-year-old brother, Bobby, pushed past them into the house, his eyes alighting on the cat.

"Cat!" yelled Bobby. "Dad, come quick!" He ran at the cat before his father, Brian, could enter the house.

"Cat?" exclaimed Brian, nearly knocking over Kate as he chased his son through the door. Bea yelped as Bobby dived at her cat, his hands grasping for its tail before it jumped away at the last minute.

"Mr. Whiskers!" gasped Bea.

"You head him off at the stairs, Dad," ordered Bobby. "I'll chase him toward you."

Bobby knocked over a lamp beside the couch as he corralled the terrified cat toward his father.

"I have him!" yelled Brian.

Mr. Whiskers paused for a moment, calculating the timing required to dash between the man's legs and up the stairs.

"I don't have him," said Brian, grabbing at air as Mr. Whiskers breezed past.

"Up the stairs, Dad! We've got him cornered!"

Bobby and Brian thundered up the staircase.

"NO ONE IS ALLOWED TO KILL MY CAT!" bellowed Bea.

She was answered by a crash that sounded suspiciously like a mattress and box spring being flipped over in an upstairs bedroom.

"BRIAN, I AM SERIOUS," she shouted.

Brian appeared sheepishly at the top of the stairs. "Aw, jeesh, Bea," he said. "We're just having a little fun."

"Torturing my cat isn't *fun*," she scolded. "This is *my* house. Leave the cat alone."

"Okay, okay," he said, walking down the stairs, Bobby in tow.

"What kind of werewolf keeps a cat for a pet, Aunt Bea?" said Bobby, sitting on a step.

"Yeah," said Brian, flashing her a grin. "You're some kind of sicko."

"I *like* cats," she replied.

Kate's mother and grandmother stood in the doorway, each with an armful of bags and bedding.

"Backlog in the living room," announced Marge, a strong-looking older woman. "Where are you going to put us all, Bea? I want to get unpacked."

"Mum, you're in my room upstairs. We'll bunk together for now," said Bea. "Brian and Lisa, you're in the other room up there."

"What about me?" came a voice from the doorway.

The party turned to see John—just a few years older than Kate, he was the only member of the group she wasn't related to. John's father had abandoned him in New Brunswick after John refused to help put Kate's family on the front page of a junky tabloid newspaper.

"John," said Bea, "you and Bobby can sleep in the living room on the pull-out couch. Sorry, it's the best I've got, given the circumstances."

"No problem," said John. He dropped his pack and bedroll on the ground beside the couch. He smiled. "Look, I'm already unpacked."

"And Katie," said Bea, eyeing her niece. "I've been thinking about what to do with you. Come with me."

Bea led Kate through the kitchen to the basement door. They walked down the steps to a room with a ceiling so low they could barely stand up. The walls were the rough concrete of the house's foundation. It smelled vaguely of dirty laundry.

"It gets better, I promise," said Bea, noticing the look on Kate's face.

A corner of the open basement was walled off with wood partitions, creating a room with a small door. The room was tiny with swept wooden floors. Shelves lining two of the walls held rows of dusty Mason jars.

"The old lady who used to live here kept all of her canned peaches and tomatoes and things in here," said Bea. "I'm pretty sure if you look hard enough, you'll find jars that date back to the fifties." Bea smiled. "But it's quiet and dry, and best of all, it's private. And it's yours if you want."

Kate looked around the room. A few rays of sunlight squeezed through the narrow window on the far wall illuminating a row of jars, their glass shining even through thick layers of dust. She dropped her bags.

"It's perfect," she announced.

# CHAPTER TWO

DIRK BRAGG PACED BACK AND FORTH IN THE HALL-
way outside the New York offices of *Really Real News*.
It had been more than a month since he'd set foot in the
newsroom. Since then, he had become the laughingstock of journalism. And for a reporter at *Really Real
News,* that was saying something.

On a journalism scale of one to ten, with *The New
York Times* at ten and *The National Enquirer* at one,
*Really Real News* was somewhere around minus fifteen.
The name Dirk Bragg had become synonymous with
ridiculous, made-up tabloid journalism.

Yesterday morning—*Was it really just yesterday?* thought Dirk—Dirk had made a now infamous
appearance on *America This Morning.* After spending a
month undercover in an abandoned house in rural New
Brunswick, Canada, Dirk had managed to witness the
amazing transformation of human beings into real,

actual, no-fooling wolves. Even more amazing—Dirk himself could still hardly believe it—one of them had turned into a *duck*. He'd taken photographs and video to prove it all. But when he arrived at a TV studio to tell the amazing story to the world...disaster. Somehow, all the evidence of werewolves (and wereduck) had vanished from his camera. In its place was a humiliating video of Dirk singing a country and western song at a karaoke bar. When it played in front of millions of people, Dirk had looked like an absolute moron.

Not that he had done a bad job at the karaoke. Dirk was rather proud of his performance. Still, in the world of journalism, Dirk Bragg had become a laughingstock.

Dirk stared at the door of the newsroom, dreading his entrance. His colleagues would be merciless. They would ridicule him. He would almost certainly be fired. And who would hire a disgraced tabloid newspaper reporter? *Really Real News* was already the lowest rung on the ladder.

Dirk closed his eyes and took a deep breath. *Let them laugh,* he thought. He knew the truth. Dirk stood up straight, checked his cowlick in the reflection of the window, and entered the newsroom.

Halfway across the room, and still nobody had noticed him. Reporters around him chatted on telephones and typed up stories.

*Just a few more paces to my desk,* thought Dirk. He could see the light on his phone was flashing. It was probably a message from his publisher notifying him of his immediate termination.

"Hey, look!" called someone a few desks over. "It's Dirk Bragg!"

*Here it comes,* thought Dirk with a wince. *Now I'll get it.*

Dirk's editor, Sandra, popped up from the other side of his desk. "Ready, everyone? One, two, three...."

Every voice in the newsroom sang together:

*"For he's a jolly good fellow,*
*For he's a jolly good fellow,*
*For he's a jolly good fel-LOOOOOOOW!*
*Which nobody can deny!"*

The newsroom rang with cheers and applause. People crowded around Dirk to shake his hand and slap him on the back.

"Nice work, Bragg!"

"Attaboy! Ace!"

"That's our Bragg!"

A group of men sang an earnest tribute to Dirk's nationally televised karaoke performance: *"My wheels belong to the road, but my heaaaart—belongs to yooooou!"*

"Way to go, Dirk!"

Someone popped the cork in a bottle of champagne and thrust a glass into his hand.

"Here's to you, Dirk!"

Dirk took a reluctant sip. He was stymied. Rather than being the embarrassment of the newsroom, he seemed to be...its hero?

Dirk sidled through the crowd of well-wishers toward Sandra, who beamed at him from the edge of the throng.

"Sandra," he muttered from the side of his mouth, "this is real nice, but why is it happening? I thought I'd be fired."

"Fired!" bellowed Sandra. "Dirk, if anything you'll get a raise!"

"That's, um, nice," Dirk began awkwardly, "but a tad inconsistent with the level of shame and embarrassment I've brought upon this news organization."

"'Shame and embarrassment'?" mocked Sandra. "You never change, Bragg. Sure, to someone who takes journalism seriously, what you did yesterday on *America This Morning* was, let's face it, a disgrace. But we're a scummy tabloid! Disgrace is what we do! We've sold more subscriptions in the last twenty-four hours than we have in the last twenty-four months!"

Dirk brightened a bit. "So, I still have a job?"

"Son, you keep embarrassing yourself on national television, and you've got a job for life," said Sandra. "Now, as your editor, I have just one request."

Dirk winced, still dreading some sort of penance. "What's that?"

"Sit down and *write that wereduck story*! This is going to be the bestselling edition in the history of the paper!" Sandra took a sip of her champagne and left Dirk to his thoughts.

Dirk nudged his way back through the crowd to his desk. He plopped into his chair, switched on his computer, and dialled into his voicemail.

"You have twenty-five new messages," began the electronic voice on the phone.

"Oh, sheesh," said Dirk, pushing a button to queue up the first message.

*BEEP.*

"Bragg! You magnificent moron!" bellowed the voice of Pete Daitch, *Really Real News*'s publisher. "My boy, you were fabulous on TV this morning. You have a bright future at this paper. What do you think of the title Senior Investigative Reporter? My secretary will set up a meeting. Heh heh. A wereduck. Priceless."

*BEEP.*

Dirk's face flushed. This day was definitely turning out better than he'd thought.

*BEEP.*

"Hello, Mr. Bragg," said a woman with a deep, sultry voice. "My name is Veronica Nightshade, and I'm a *big* fan of the idea of people who become *dangerous* animals by the light of the moon. I saw you on *America This Morning*, and I, uh, thought you looked like someone I would like to get to know."

Before the message ended, Veronica Nightshade left her phone number and made a sort of growling sound. Dirk blushed and cued up the next message.

*BEEP.*

"Mr. Bragg? This is Julie Mountain with B&M Records. I'm going to cut to the chase. I thought your performance on *America This Morning* was inspired. I'm prepared to offer you a recording contract. That *voice.* That *presence.* I think you've got the makings of a star. Call me. Soon."

*BEEP.*

Dirk sank into his chair in ecstasy. Yes, today was turning out just fine.

# CHAPTER THREE

KATE CLIMBED THE BASEMENT STAIRS THE NEXT
morning to find her grandmother the only person up
and about. She moved around the kitchen as if she'd
worked in the space her entire life. The table was set.
A pot of oatmeal burbled on the stove.

"Good morning," said Kate.

"Morning," said Marge, automatically pouring
Kate a cup of tea.

"You're the best," she replied, taking the cup and
blowing steam from its surface.

"It's awfully nice to be back in a proper kitchen,"
said Marge, filling a bowl with oatmeal from the pot.
"I don't mind running a camp kitchen, but it sure is
wonderful to have a stove again." She switched one of
the gas burners on and off. "I swear, it's magic."

Kate sat at the table, sipping her drink. She looked
around the table at the place settings.

"You're missing a spot, Grandma," she said. "There are seven of us. You've only set places for six."

"John's already eaten and gone. He cleaned up his own dishes and set the table for the rest of us before I even rolled out of bed," said Marge. "He even made the oatmeal. I have to say, I like that boy more and more."

"Gone?" said Kate. "Where'd he go this early?"

"Not sure," said Marge.

"Shouldn't he be, like, careful?" said Kate. "Who knows who could be out there looking for us?"

"John's a big boy," said Marge. "I'm sure he wouldn't do anything foolish."

"Dirt Bag already found us once," said Kate. "And who knows where Marcus is."

"Deep breaths, Kate," said her grandmother flatly as she poured cold milk on her oatmeal. "He'll be careful."

Kate slumped in her chair.

"Oatmeal!" exclaimed Bea as she entered the kitchen with Kate's mother, Lisa. "The table's set already? Ma, I should have invited you to live with me *years* ago." She kissed her mother on the top of her head.

"And I would have come," said Marge. "But don't thank me. This is all John's handiwork."

"John?" said Bea, scooping oatmeal into a bowl. "I like that boy."

Kate rolled her eyes and took another sip of tea. "What are you doing today, Mum?"

"I'm not sure," said Lisa, settling in beside Kate. "I suppose I ought to find a way to make myself useful. I hate the idea of twiddling my thumbs around here."

"Oh, my gosh!" exclaimed Bea. "Come to work with me at the construction site. It would be so fun."

"I don't know," said Lisa. "I haven't swung a hammer in years."

"Don't be ridiculous," said Bea. "You're a better carpenter than half the journeymen at that site. I'll just introduce you to my boss, and you're in."

"Do it, Mum," said Kate. "You know you'd love it."

"For sure!" said Bea. "And it's all under-the-table payment, so it's perfect. It's like we don't even exist. I take every full moon off, and nobody bats an eye. They all think I'm some sort of pagan moon-worshipper or something."

Lisa laughed. "Well, okay. I'll give it a try," she said. "If you think."

"I *think,*" said Bea. "It's settled."

Brian walked groggily into the kitchen and filled a bowl from the pot on the stove. He settled across the table from Kate and took a bite.

"Excellent oatmeal, Marge," he said, chewing thoughtfully. "Better than usual. Just a hint of cinnamon."

"John made it," said Marge.

"John?" said Brian. He lifted his spoon to his mouth and took another bite. "I like that boy."

"Everybody does, apparently," muttered Kate.

"Kate, you've *got* to try this," said Lisa.

"Mm, I'm not that hungry," said Kate. She grabbed a slice of toast from the middle of the table and scraped butter across its dry surface.

# CHAPTER FOUR

KATE AND BOBBY'S DAD GAVE THEM THE DAY OFF from home-school lessons to settle into their new home. Kate spent her morning cleaning her new room. She hauled everything out before sweeping the floor and scrubbing decades of dust from every surface. She emptied seven buckets of scummy water out the back door as her cleaning sponge uncovered the raw wood of the walls and floor. A bit of vinegar and hot water cleared up the window, revealing the swirls and hazy sections that showed the glass to be as old as the house itself.

After a morning of work, Kate stood in the doorway and surveyed her progress. The grey layers of dust were gone, replaced by the warm brown of unfinished wood panelling and shelves. The room smelled of clean, damp wood.

"Better," she said aloud.

It took several trips up and down the basement stairs to bring all the empty jars to the kitchen for cleaning. A few hidden in the back rows, indeed, still had food in them, though not as old as Aunt Bea had suspected. The earliest artefact was a jar of mustard pickles labelled "*Summer 1984.*" Kate washed each empty jar and laid them out on towels to dry. She hid the full ones at the back of the cereal cupboard.

Bobby breezed through the back door into the kitchen. He was covered from head to toe in muck and mud, a fact he seemed oblivious to as he grabbed a stack of cookies from a jar on the counter with his grubby hand.

"What are you looking for?" he asked.

Kate stood on a chair, peering into the upper row of cupboards. She pushed items aside to see to the back.

"Food colouring," she said. "I'm sure Bea's got food colouring somewhere."

"What for?" asked Bobby.

"I need it for my room," she answered, opening the door to another cupboard.

"Your room needs...food colouring?" he asked.

Kate lowered her eyes to look at him. He was filthy and was shoving the filth into his mouth by way of the now-filthy cookies.

She narrowed her eyes. "Go away," she said.

"I was just asking," he said. He grabbed a fresh handful of cookies and stomped out of the house. "We're out here working on *your* thing, y'know."

Kate stood on the chair and watched the door slam behind her brother. What exactly could they be working on for her?

She spotted a familiar box at the back of the top shelf. She grabbed the food colouring and placed it on the counter before following Bobby outside.

She found him with her father, who was covered in an equal amount of filth. Brian was digging a giant hole in the backyard with a spade. He looked up from his work and smiled.

"Aw, this was supposed to be a surprise," he said, wiping sweat from his forehead with the back of his work glove. "You caught us."

"Wow, Dad," said Kate flatly, surveying his work. "It's really lovely. This hole. In the ground."

"It's more for Wacka, really," he said, grabbing a dirty cookie from Bobby and taking a bite.

Kate smiled as she realized what she was looking at.

"A pond," she said. "Dad, it's great!"

"Still quite a bit of work left, but it should be nice and homey by the time we're done," said Brian. "Your grandma is out looking for bulrushes to plant around the edges."

"It's perfect, Dad," Kate said. "Really. Wacka is going to love it."

"I'm not so sure about that," said Bobby, pointing toward one of the lawn chairs by the back door. There sat Wacka, the female mallard duck they'd brought all the way from New Brunswick. Wacka rested with her eyes closed, prim and proper, absorbing the rays of the sun. "We already made her a nest, but she's not interested."

"I swear that duck thinks she's human," laughed Brian, shaking his head.

Kate kneeled at Wacka's side and stroked her feathers. "Wacka," she whispered. "Look, your bandages are gone." Kate shuddered as she thought of the awful attack from Marcus—John's father—that had nearly killed the little duck. Two matching red scabs showed the spot where he'd bit her. Now that the swelling was down, they didn't look nearly as bad as they had a few days earlier. Even her feathers were looking better.

"Your grandma looked her over this morning and said the bite marks are healing really well," said Brian. "She didn't think Wacka needed the bandages anymore. This little duck is going to be fine."

"That's great news, Wacka," said Kate. She beamed at her friend.

"I suppose you'll both be spending some time paddling around our little pond sooner or later," said Brian.

Kate smiled. "Thanks, Dad. This looks really great."

She turned and walked toward the house.

"Hold up!" called Brian. "Looks like someone wants to come with you."

Kate turned and saw Wacka struggling to lift herself from her chair. The injured duck was having a hard time, but seemed determined to follow.

"Where do you think you're going?" asked Kate.

"Wacka," said the duck weakly.

"Oh my gosh. You're the sweetest thing," said Kate, lifting the duck into her arms and cradling her like a newborn. "Of course you can come in with me. I'll fix up a corner of my room just for you."

"Wacka."

# CHAPTER FIVE

AFTER SEVERAL HOURS OF PILLAGING AUNT BEA'S Christmas decorations and arranging and cleaning, Kate proclaimed her bedroom ready to be lived in. She bounded up the basement steps to the kitchen. She was greeted by a summer harvest feast laid out on the table.

"Holy cow," she announced, gaping at the plates of sliced ripe tomatoes and peppers, and steaming platters of corn on the cob and new potatoes. "Where'd all this come from?"

Her father set a plate of cucumber slices on the table. "Seems our good pal John here spent his day getting a job on a farm," said Brian. He looked at John, the only person seated at the table, already tucked into the meal.

"*Mfflpomm,*" said John through a mouthful of potato. He finished chewing and swallowed. "They're paying me in cash and whatever produce I can carry home."

DAVE ATKINSON

"They're paying him in food!" exclaimed Brian, not even trying to hide his giddiness. He placed a hand on John's shoulder. "Son—can I call you son?—you can stay with us as long as you like."

John blushed. "It's the least I could do."

He speared another potato with his fork.

"Actually," said Brian with a smirk, "Kate demonstrates right now the actual least you could do. This pile of food officially makes you my favourite child."

"*Dad*," said Kate, glaring at her father.

"What?" he said.

"What happened to a little thing called 'keeping a low profile'?" she asked. "Haven't we, for our *entire lives*, been hiding so that no one will find us? Someone like, oh, say, Dirk Bragg the *Dirt Bag*? Or even *Marcus*?"

John winced at the mention of his father.

Brian sighed. "Yes," he said finally. "But Dirt Bag has no way of tracking us. We were gone by the time he could have made it back to our camp. And Marcus—well, no one ever told Marcus where Bea lived. Including Bea. So, for now—so long as we're still careful—I think we're okay."

"But what about everyone else?" said Kate. "What about people at the farm where John's working?"

"Well," said John, sprinkling a bit of salt on a slice of tomato, "I do this thing that helps me blend in with the rest of the people. I don't howl."

"Ha ha," said Kate dryly.

"What?" said John. "My dad always said that sometimes the best place to hide is right in plain sight."

"Ah, yes," said Kate. "Your dad. That fountain of backstabbing, duck-biting wisdom."

For a moment, it was as if Kate had dropped a bomb in the room. All was silent as she and John glared at each other across the table.

Brian finally coughed. "So, uh, Kate," he began awkwardly. "What did you do all day while John was busy filling our table with this glorious feast?" he asked.

Kate glared at John for a moment longer before looking at her father. "I was just going to say I just finished—"

John's chair scraped across the kitchen floor as he pushed back from the table.

"I gotta run," he said, wiping his mouth on a napkin and standing up.

"Run? You just got home from work," said Brian. "Where could you possibly have to go?"

"The library closes at six-thirty," said John, rinsing his dishes in the sink.

"The *library*?" said Kate.

"Yeah, you know," said John. "The place with the books?"

Brian laughed.

Kate scrunched her brow. "What are you doing at the library?"

"There's just some stuff I want to look up," he replied.

"You hear that?" said Brian to his daughter. "He has *stuff*. Stuff he wants to *look up*. At the *library*." He prodded her playfully. "Why don't *you* ever go to the library?"

"Because they invented the internet," said Kate. She glared at John. "And I don't need to show off."

John slung his backpack over his shoulder. He hesitated a moment at the front door. "I'm not trying to show off to anybody," he said quietly. "I'll be back in a bit."

"Take your time," said Brian as John walked out the door. He stared at Kate.

"What?" she said.

"What was that?" he asked. "His dad abandoned him three days ago and now *he's* the one taking care of *us*."

"Whatever," said Kate. She put a piece of corn and a handful of cucumber slices on her plate before heading to the basement door. "If you need me, I'll be in my room doing the least I can do."

# CHAPTER SIX

MARCUS CREPT THROUGH THE SHADOWS ALONG A country laneway. It was well after midnight. A faint breeze rustled the leaves of the trees above him. Not a car stirred on the lonely stretch of gravel just a hundred metres away.

The small farmhouse was dark. A single flickering bulb hanging from a pole faintly illuminated the barnyard. Marcus watched from the shadows in front of the house before making his move.

A car and pickup truck sat parked in the driveway. Marcus approached the car and tried the handle on the driver's side.

Unlocked. Perfect.

He opened the door and slid into the driver's seat. He reached under the seat, looking for keys. Nothing. He opened the glove box. It was stuffed to overflowing with old registration papers and tissues. He checked above the sun visor. No luck.

And then he noticed a set of keys dangling from the ignition. He smiled.

"Unlocked doors and keys left in the ignition," Marcus said to himself as he started the car. "I love country folk."

He put the car into gear and drove slowly down the lane with the lights turned off. Marcus didn't like stealing. He really didn't. But it was necessary for a werewolf to keep moving. He'd learned too many times that staying in one spot was dangerous. Making friends was dangerous. Just look where it got him this time.

He'd tried to lower his guard and learn to trust. He'd even, for a few weeks, thought maybe he could build a home with his son, John, and Bea. Bea's family had lived at that camp in rural New Brunswick for nearly a decade without being noticed. Maybe he could have done the same.

But it was all a lie he'd told himself. Werewolves are never safe. Hand your trust to anyone and they will crush it like a dead leaf. Just like Bea did. Just like John's mother did.

*Laura.*

He hadn't seen her in more than fifteen years, but the thought of her was still like a punch to the gut. *She* was the reason Marcus and John had begun their nomadic life in the first place: always moving, always running. If John were to find out the truth—that his mother was still alive—if he were to seek her out....

Marcus shuddered.

He would just have to make sure that never happened. He didn't know exactly where John was, but Bea had let slip enough details about where she lived that Marcus could narrow his search. He'd find them soon enough.

# CHAPTER SEVEN

KATE WAS LYING ON HER BED, STARING AT THE ceiling, when a knock came at her door.

"Go away," she said.

"Come on," said John, his voice muffled by the door between them. "I just want to talk to you."

Kate didn't answer.

"Can I come in?" pleaded John.

"I can't stop you."

The door opened a crack. John peered in.

"Hey, listen. I don't know what's going on with you, but—*holy cow, what'd you do to your room?*"

John stood in the doorway, his mouth agape. He glanced around the room. "This is...amazing."

Kate looked around. The rows of Mason jars were now clean and filled with water tinted varying shades of blue and green. She had pilfered Aunt Bea's Christmas decorations and strung lights behind each row of jars.

The light shimmered through the coloured liquid to give the whole room a feeling of being under water.

"Hey, you made Wacka her own place, too," exclaimed John. "You didn't miss a thing!"

Wacka paddled quietly in a small inflatable kiddie pool behind the door. Kate had planted long grass and bulrushes dug up from a nearby ditch in pots and set them around the pool. The little duck looked quite at home.

"I found the pool stuffed in a box," explained Kate with a shrug. As resentful as she felt toward John, she couldn't help being proud of how she'd transformed her room.

John sat at the end of her bed. "Are you mad at me?"

Kate put her hands behind her head and looked at the ceiling. She'd thought about that question for the last couple of hours, but she still couldn't find the right words to explain how she felt.

"Things just feel stupid, you know?" she said.

"What kind of stupid?"

"Like, they're not supposed to be like this. *We're* not supposed to be here. *You're* not supposed to be here," she said.

"But we *are* here," he said. "I *am* here."

"It's hard enough having to pick up my whole life—which was perfectly great before you and your dad came along—and move it to boring Ontario," said Kate. "And you have to go and make it harder by being Mr. Perfect Son."

John scowled. Kate had struck a nerve. She didn't realize what she was going to say until she had already said it. But it was exactly how she felt. Right or wrong, this whole dumb situation seemed like John's fault.

"Wow," said John, his eyes flaring. "Wow." He shook his head.

Several seconds passed as both waited for the other to say something.

"That's it, huh?" said Kate. "Just 'wow'?"

"I guess so," he said. John stood to walk out. He paused a moment with his hand on the doorknob. "Cool room," he said, closing the door behind him.

# CHAPTER EIGHT

KATE SAT AT THE KITCHEN TABLE FLIPPING through index cards in her grandmother's recipe box. Wacka watched from her perch on the chair next to her as Bobby skipped into the room.

"Eleven-year-olds don't skip," said Kate without looking up.

"Huh," said Bobby. He paused a moment, looking concerned, then skipped gleefully around the kitchen table. "Well, look at that," said Bobby, mid-skip. "Looks like you're *wrong*, Ms. Ducky."

Kate smiled. "Sorry," she said. "I've been a bit of a grump the last couple of weeks."

"Man, I'm used to it," said Bobby, plopping into a chair across the table. "What are you doing?"

"I was looking for Grandma's cake recipe," said Kate, flipping back through the cards.

"What for?"

"Can't a girl just do something nice for her family?" she said.

Bobby looked around. "Who, you mean *you*?"

"Shut up," she said with a grin. Her eyes fell on the title of a weathered index card near the back of the box. The handwriting was in an old-fashioned, spidery script that was not her grandmother's. "What's this?"

"What?" said Bobby, leaning in.

"'A Cure for Werewolf,'" she read. She looked at her brother. "What the heck does that mean?" She scanned the ingredients on the card. "Yuck. There's a lot of weird stuff in here."

"What is it?"

"'A rest from the monthly lunar madness,'" read Kate. She paused, mulling over the card. "I think this is a temporary cure for being a werewolf."

"Weird," said her brother. "Why would someone want to do that?"

"I don't know," said Kate. "Not everyone likes being a wolf, I guess. Let's go find Grandma."

Wacka gave a little quack as Kate scooped her up and led Bobby outside. They found Marge hanging laundry in the sun.

"Grandma," said Kate. "We found something in your recipe box."

Marge smacked her lips. "Banana bread?" she said, pinning one end of a bedsheet to the clothesline. "Sounds great. I encourage you to make it."

"Ha," replied Bobby. "Seriously. 'Cure for Werewolf.' What's that all about?"

Marge's eyes brightened as she dropped a wet towel back into the basket. "You found that? Let me see." She took the card from Kate and looked it over. "I haven't seen this in years," she said. "That's your great-great-grandmother's handwriting, did you know that? I've been meaning to re-copy it. See how faded it's become?"

"Yeah, but what is it? Is it for real?" asked Kate.

"My granny swore it worked, but she never made it herself," said Marge. "Mum and I always thought it was a bit of a joke. I wouldn't worry about it."

"Why don't you think it works?" asked Kate.

"Oh, I don't know one way or another, but if there was a cure for werewolves—even a temporary one—I think we'd know about it," said Marge. "I think this is just a bit of superstitious nonsense. Look," she said, tapping the card, "a couple of these ingredients would be nearly impossible to find anyway."

"Like what?" asked Bobby.

Marge thumbed the card. "Well, actually, some of these are just old-fashioned names for wild herbs. Like this: beggar's buttons. That's just burdock. But it says here it has to be harvested 'under a waning moon,'" she chuckled, reading down the list. "And then there's the poem at the end:

*If the wolf you seek to calm,*
*Let this potion be your guide:*
*A shot of silver, a soothing balm;*
*Still the beast that lives inside.*

"It just sounds made-up to me," she said.

"Does most of the stuff grow around here?" asked Kate.

Marge read through the card. "Well, I think most of it would, if you know where to look. Loostrife you might have trouble with. That's European, unless it came here as an invasive species. Kronos's blood? I couldn't even begin to guess what *that* is. And silver nitrate. Pretty sure you'd have to visit a nineteenth-century apothecary for that one." She handed the card back to Kate. "I'd just hate to see you go to all the trouble for nothing."

"Thanks," said Kate, deflating.

Kate walked back to the kitchen and slid the recipe card behind the others in the box on the kitchen table. Then she paused a moment. She didn't mind her new life as a wereduck, but the promise of being able to turn it on and off was intriguing.

She pulled it back out.

It couldn't hurt to try.

# CHAPTER NINE

JOHN DROPPED A BAG OF SWEET CORN ON THE kitchen counter as he walked into the house after a day of work. He was about to walk into the living room but stopped short. Kate stood in the doorway, blocking his path.

"Hey," she said.

"Hey," he said, attempting to walk around her. She stepped to the side, still blocking his way.

"Hey," she repeated.

"I'm trying to get my bag so I can go to the library."

"Right. I know." She glanced at the ceiling and took a breath. "I was wondering if I could, y'know, come with you."

He stepped around her and grabbed his bag. "You don't need my permission."

"And I was wondering," she continued, swivelling to face him, "if maybe, you might, y'know, help me find some stuff."

John stood back a moment and stared at her. "But that would, *y'know*, require *talking* to me," said John. "Which, *y'know*, I didn't think you did anymore."

"Well, maybe I need your help looking up some stuff," said Kate. She looked at the floor. "And maybe I haven't been the nicest to you since we got here."

John raised his eyebrows. "Maybe," he said.

"And maybe," she said, "maybe I'm sorry about that."

"Huh," said John, considering. "Well, what do you need me for? I thought that's why they invented the internet."

"Well, what I'm looking for doesn't seem to be on it."

"Okay," he said, relaxing slightly. "So what exactly are you looking for?"

"This," she said. Kate dug a piece of paper from her pocket and handed it to John. "I have a list of old names for wild herbs and plants. I want to know what they really are and where I can find them."

John took the paper. "Okay," he said. "Why do you need that?"

"Do you really need to know?" asked Kate.

"Not really," he said, slinging his bag over his shoulder. "I was just curious about how far you'd go with, *y'know*, talking."

John and Kate stood in front of the card files in the old, small-town library. John's fingers flipped through the long drawer of index cards.

"*Herbs of Europe, Wildflowers of Western Canada, The Big Book of British Herbs...*" read John. "These don't seem to be what you're looking for."

Kate stood with her arms crossed. "Is that it? They don't have anything on the plants that grow around here?"

"Not that I can find," he said, sliding the drawer back into place. "But if it's here, I bet Marty can find it."

"Who's Marty?"

John brightened. "He's the librarian. He's awesome. Come on."

The two walked to the front of the library, where a skinny man with greying hair was copying dates into a ledger. He was so focused on his task, he didn't notice the two teens approach.

"Hey, Marty," whispered John.

The man jolted to attention, dropping his pencil. "John!" he exclaimed at the top of his lungs. "You nearly scared me to death! How are you today? You brought a friend! How nice." He thrust his hand at Kate. "I'm Marty."

Kate shook his offered hand. She introduced herself. "Aren't we supposed to be quiet in a library?"

"Well, right now, there are exactly three people in this library," began Marty, glancing around, "and darn it if all of them aren't standing right here. I think we can safely chat without disturbing anyone."

Kate blushed. She liked this man's easy way.

"Marty, we're trying to find a book about local wild plants and herbs," said John. "Have you got anything?"

"Got anything!" Marty waved his hands and clasped them in front of his heart. "I've the *perfect* book. To the local section!"

Marty dashed toward a back corner of the library, leaving Kate and John to scurry after. He stopped in front of a small set of shelves.

"This is where we hide—sorry, *keep*—the books written by local authors. We occasionally get someone who wrote their family history or a book of bad poetry and drops off a copy. They're usually dreadful, but in your case, you want Muriel Tuttle's book. It's charming. A real peach."

Marty's fingers skimmed the spines on the shelf. "Got it," he said, grabbing a book bound with yellowed canvas. He handed it to Kate. "*Local Flora.* Probably my favourite book in the whole library. Treat it gently."

Kate opened it and gingerly leafed through a few pages. The book didn't seem so special to her; its pages were filled with sparse, handwritten text and simple illustrations of plants.

"It's nice," she lied.

"Nice?" exclaimed Marty, yanking the book from her hands. "Look at this." He flipped to the page titled "Dandelion." It was illustrated with a simple ink drawing of a dandelion, with neat, handwritten text beneath. "This lady spent her whole life hiking through every forest and hedgerow in this county with a sketchbook under her arm. She'd spend entire days drawing and re-drawing illustrations of every plant—even simple, everyday things like dandelions—to get them perfect. And look at this." His finger traced the writing beneath the picture. "Latin name. Common name. Folk name. Common uses. Where it grows. It's just perfect."

Kate attempted to match Marty's enthusiasm with a smile. "That's really neat."

Marty looked dreamily into the distance as he continued. "She brought it in about twenty years ago when I had just started working here as a shelver. Tiny old lady—she was so shy about it. Came in and said she'd written a book and wondered if we'd like it. We *always* say yes, no matter how bad it is, but this is just a work of genius. Written and illustrated completely by hand. I must have chatted with her for hours. I'm afraid I embarrassed her with my gushing."

"Sounds exactly like what you need, Kate," said John.

She nodded.

"Y'know," said Marty, lost in his own train of thought, "I asked her if she'd tried sending it to a publisher, but she wasn't interested. She just wanted to record the plants that grow within fifteen kilometres of her house. And she'd never travelled farther than that herself in her *whole life*. Like a modern-day Kant. Amazing, isn't it? She dropped it off that day, and I never saw her again."

He tapped the book against his chin and noticed Kate and John staring at him.

"Sorry," he said. "Got a bit carried away there."

He walked them back to the front desk where he scratched a few details into his ledger. He stamped the slip in the back of the book and handed it to Kate. "Take care of it. It's the only copy."

"Like, *only* copy?" said Kate.

"She wrote it, bound it, and brought it here as a gift to the library. It's the only copy that I know of."

"Wow," marvelled Kate. "Thanks."

"Oh, and John," said Marty. "I had another delivery from the central library." He hefted a small cardboard box filled with dozens of spools of what looked like miniature movie film from below the desk.

Kate raised her eyebrows. "What's that?"

"Microfilm," explained Marty. "It's just what it sounds like: tiny film. This is how we kept record of old newspapers before we could digitize them, which, unfortunately, is still something we can't afford to do at our little library. These spools have hundreds of issues on them." He turned to John. "I'll leave it here for whenever you need it."

"Oh, great," said John, shifting his weight from one foot to the other. Kate thought he looked a little bit nervous. "Thanks."

The two walked out of the library a few minutes later, Kate with the yellow book under her arm.

"What's with the microfilm?" she asked. "Are you some sort of 1980s secret agent or something?"

"Ha. It's nothing."

"No, seriously. What's it for?"

"Nothing," he snapped. "It's just some stuff I'm looking up. It's not a big deal."

"If it's not a big deal, why not tell me—"

"All right," he said, looking straight ahead. "First tell me why we were looking up all those old weeds."

Kate squirmed. She didn't want to confess about the cure. What if he laughed? She wasn't ready to bring him in on this secret. Not yet.

She shrugged. "It's just something I'm interested in."

"Okay," said John. "Well then, I guess I'm just interested in microfilm."

Kate sighed. The truce wasn't going well.

# CHAPTER TEN

DIRK'S FOOT TAPPED NERVOUSLY AS HE WATCHED the floor numbers tick by in the elevator. He looked at his watch. He was already five minutes late for his interview.

"Dang."

The button for Dirk's floor was already lit, but he jabbed at it repeatedly anyway.

A bell dinged. The elevator stopped to let on a new passenger: a young woman with a newspaper tucked under her arm. Dirk nodded a curt greeting.

He stared again at the floor numbers, willing them to move faster. After a few floors, he couldn't help but notice out of the corner of his eye that the woman was staring at him.

"Can I help you?" he asked.

"I'm sorry," she stammered, "but aren't you Dirk Bragg? The reporter?"

Dirk looked at her. The woman was in her mid-twenties. Dirk could now see the newspaper in her hand was, in fact, a copy of *Really Real News*—the very issue with his story about the wereduck.

Dirk chuffed. "Why, yes," he said. "Yes, I am."

The woman blushed. "I thought that was you," she said shyly. "I just think your work at *Really Real News* is…." She paused a moment, searching for a strong enough word. "Amazing."

"Well," said Dirk, trying to look modest. "I don't know about *amazing*, but—"

"No, really," she gushed. "I just think you're a genius. You're probably pretty busy, but—gosh—would you mind signing my newspaper?"

She thrust it at him.

"I'm on my way to an important radio interview," said Dirk, "but sure. Anything for a fan."

He plucked a pen from his shirt pocket.

"Great," she said. "Can you make it out to Karen?"

"Sure thing," he said, scribbling her name.

"My friends will absolutely flip out that I met you," said Karen. "We just think you've taken outrageous, made-up news to another level. I mean, where do you come up with this stuff? It's absolutely preposterous and embarrassing, but you write it so sincerely—like you actually seem to believe it."

Dirk's face flushed. "Well, I wouldn't say I, uh—"

"No, I mean it," she said. "This wereduck story? It's so absurd that it's perfect. And there are idiots out there who actually think it's true!"

"Gosh, um, Karen. I really think you should consider—" said Dirk.

"And when you were on *America This Morning*?" said Karen. "When you sang that stupid song? It was like performance art."

The elevator bell dinged again.

"Oh, that's my floor," said Karen. "Thanks, Mr. Bragg." She gave him a hug, which he reluctantly returned. "Keep up the amazing work."

She stepped out of the elevator. The doors shut. Dirk's mouth didn't.

"We're going to go right to the phone lines," said the radio host sitting across the dimly lit studio from Dirk. "We have a number of callers waiting to speak with Dirk Bragg, the senior investigative reporter for *Really Real News*. The man who witnessed, with his own eyes, evidence of werewolves—and a wereduck. Our first caller is Bill from Des Moines. What's your question for Dirk Bragg, Bill?"

"Oh, hi," came a voice over the studio phone lines. "Wow, I can't believe I made it through. Mr. Bragg, I saw you on *America This Morning* and read your article in the paper. Great stuff."

"Why thank you, Bill," said Dirk, adjusting his headphones. He smiled. "That's kind of you to say."

"What's your question for Dirk?" repeated the host.

"Right," said Bill. "I was wondering, how do you keep a straight face when you're presenting this non-sense to the country? I mean, it's so convincing. It's like you actually *believe* this garbage."

Dirk cleared his throat.

"Great question, Bill," said the host. "Dirk?"

"Well, it's simple," said Dirk, a little defensively. "I have no problem keeping a straight face because it's true. Every word."

The line was quiet for an awkward moment before both Bill and the host broke out laughing.

"You really are remarkable," laughed Bill. "One of the greats. Thanks for the laugh!"

The host chuckled. "Thanks, Bill. Our next caller is Jan in Seattle. What's your question for Dirk Bragg?"

"Hi, Mr. Bragg," said a woman's voice. "When you're inventing a crazy story for your, um, *newspaper*, do you first—"

"Hold on," interrupted Dirk. "I'm a bit confused." Dirk faced the host. "Is the whole pretence of this interview that I'm...making up news stories? That I'm a fraud?"

The host shifted nervously in his chair. "Well, I don't know if 'fraud' is the right word, Dirk, but...."

Dirk was indignant. "Maybe you prefer the term 'phoney,' then? Or how about 'fake'?"

"We're going to take a quick commercial break," said the host, effortlessly shifting back into his friendly announcer voice, "but we'll be right back with more questions for Dirk Bragg."

The host yanked off his headphones the second a life insurance commercial began.

"Dirk, I don't know what to say here—I mean, you do work for *Really Real News*," said the host.

"And that automatically means I write untrue stories, does it?" said Dirk. "Am I a joke to you?"

"Okay, I see what's going on here," said the host with a nod. He glanced at the clock. There was less than a minute before the commercial break ended. "Dirk, I'm going to be straight with you, because you seem like a nice guy. You're a rising star. You are going to be super huge, if you play this whole thing right. But the thing you have to understand is that you're not famous for exposing the secret world of werewolves."

"But—" began Dirk.

"Seventeen seconds," warned the host, tapping his watch. "Dirk, people love you because they think you've taken crazy and cranked it up a notch. They think you're making fun of newspapers like *Really Real News* from the *inside*."

"But I—"

"Dirk," interrupted the host, putting his headphones back on. "Just go for it, man. Let them love you! Enjoy the ride." The host flipped a switch to turn on his mic. "Welcome back! We're going straight to the phone lines for Dirk Bragg. Libby in Dallas, what's your question for Dirk?"

"Aaaah, I can't believe I made it through!" said Libby. "Mr. Bragg, can you sing that song for us? That wheels on the road song? I love that song!"

"Whaddaya say, Dirk?" said the host, as the opening notes of a country song began in the background. "Give it a go? For your fans?"

Dirk closed his eyes and let out a long breath.

"Sure," he said finally. "Anything for a fan."

# CHAPTER ELEVEN

"OKAY, I'M GOING TO GO OVER THIS ONE LAST time," announced Bea. The entire household—her sister's family, her mum, and John—sat at the kitchen table in the early evening. The full moon was low on the horizon out the window. The sun would set in less than an hour. They'd been living here with Bea for a month.

"This isn't the backwoods of New Brunswick," continued Bea. "This is farmland Ontario. Tonight, when you become wolves—"

"Or ducks," interjected Kate.

"Or ducks," acknowledged Bea, nodding politely. "If you dare let out one howl—"

"Or quack," said Kate, grinning widely.

"Or *quack*," said Bea. "There *are* neighbours nearby. They *will* hear you. They *will* freak out. They *will* dial 911. Understand?"

The group nodded. All but John.

"How do we answer the call of the moon without howling?" he asked.

"That's the only exception. But we will answer the call *very quietly*," said Bea, eyeing Brian, who had a special fondness for howling very loudly. "I think we should restrict ourselves to the forest on my neighbour's farm, which is just about as far away from anyone as you can get around here. Which, I will say again, is *still not very far*. Got it?"

"Got it," said Brian, nodding earnestly with the rest of the group. "And what about Mr. Whiskers? Can he come out and play?"

Bobby laughed.

"*The cat is locked in my bedroom*," said Bea, waving a finger in his face. "No cat, Brian. No cat."

Brian pouted.

"What about me?" asked Bobby. "Can I come?"

"I don't think so, sweetie," answered his mother. "I think we'd have a hard time explaining to the neighbours why an eleven-year-old boy is out prowling the woods at night. Best stay here."

Bobby deflated. He remained at his spot at the table as the rest of the group got up like soldiers dismissed at the end of a briefing session. Bobby watched quietly as his family prepared to head into the woods.

"If it helps, I'll try not to have *too* much fun," said John, patting Bobby on the head.

"Great," said Bobby, watching the group file out the back door and into the growing darkness of the evening.

Kate was the last to leave. She paused in the doorway. "Hey, do you mind checking on Wacka for me before you go to bed? She was sleeping in my room, but she may want to spend a few hours in the pond tonight."

"Sure," said Bobby. He crossed his arms as the door shut behind his sister.

Bobby slid off his chair and wandered into the living room. He plopped on the couch and turned on the TV. He flipped mindlessly through channels, never sticking to one for more than a few seconds. He cycled through every station on the dial before switching it off and throwing the remote on the couch beside him. He let out a slow breath and closed his eyes.

Wacka woke with a start. She looked around. She had been sleeping in her nest in Kate's bedroom. The room was dark but for a bit of fading light through the basement window.

Wacka stood up and stretched her wings and neck. She shook off the stiffness in her legs and stepped into the cool water of her pool.

*What an odd night,* the duck thought to herself. Odd, too, because she realized she had expressed that thought in her head with actual words. The more time she spent with Kate and her family, the more their human words seemed to make sense. As time went on, she even found herself using them herself in her own little duck head.

Tonight, she was feeling off. Anxious. And a bit excited.

Wacka couldn't figure out where these feelings were coming from. She paddled in a small circle and nibbled the tips of the pond grass at the edge of the pool.

The last bit of dusky light in the room faded as the sun dipped below the horizon. Wacka felt a wave of cold energy ripple through her body.

She jumped in fright as she heard an unfamiliar voice. Deep and resonant, it seemed to be calling her, as if from the Earth itself.

*"Whooooo?"*

# CHAPTER TWELVE

BOBBY JERKED AWAKE AND RUBBED HIS FACE. HE couldn't have been asleep for more than a few minutes.

He got up from the couch, wandered into the kitchen, and pulled open the refrigerator. Bobby stared at its contents for a full minute. He wasn't really hungry, but he broke off a piece of cheese and put it in his mouth before closing the door.

Another boring full-moon night spent at home. He looked out the window and saw the sun had already set. By now, Kate would be a duck, the rest would be wolves, and he was still boring old Bobby, stuck in this boring old farmhouse. It would be a bit more than a year before he turned thirteen and became a werewolf himself, but right now that seemed like forever away.

He heard faint noises from downstairs. A small thump. A rustling.

"Right," he said out loud. "Wacka."

Bobby thundered down the basement stairs. He could hear frantic movement from inside Kate's bedroom.

*That duck must really want to go outside,* he thought.

"I'm coming, Wacka," he said as he grabbed the door handle to his sister's room. "Keep your shirt on...."

Bobby froze in the open doorway. The room was dark, but there was no mistaking the silhouette of a person standing in the kiddie pool. Before Bobby had a chance to scream, the person began to make horrifying sounds of its own.

"WHAH-WHAH!" it screamed in a girl's voice. "WHAH-WHAH!"

The girl stepped from the pool, dripping dirty pond water on the floor as she rushed to wrap herself in the quilt on Kate's bed.

Bobby flipped on the lights. The terrified eyes of a sopping wet teenage girl stared back at him. Even beneath the tightly wrapped quilt, Bobby could tell she was shivering with cold. Her teeth chattered. Clumps of wet brown hair dripped streams of water down her face.

"WHAH-WHAH!" she repeated.

Bobby took a small step forward. "Hey, it's okay," he said gently, raising his hands. "I'm not going to hurt you."

"WHAH-WHAAAA!" said the girl more urgently.

"I don't know what you're saying," said Bobby. "Look, calm down. Why don't you just tell me your name?"

Her eyes widened. She took a deep breath. "WHAH-WHAH," she said.

"I don't understand what you're trying to say. What's 'whah-whah'?"

The girl rushed forward, her eyes wild. She pointed to the kiddie pool. "WHAH-WHAH!" she cried. She pointed to the duck's nest in the corner. "WHAH-WHAH!" she said. She pointed to herself. "WHAH-WHAH!"

Bobby stepped back. He didn't understand. It didn't make sense.

Then, all of a sudden, it made perfect sense.

He turned to the girl. "*Wacka*?" he said. "Wacka, what happened to you?"

# CHAPTER THIRTEEN

WACKA'S WILD EYES FLARED WITH JOY. "MORE!" she cried, shoving the last bit of an apple into her mouth. "MORE!"

Bobby rushed around the kitchen. "Just a sec!" he laughed, putting together a small feast for his ravenous friend. "I'm coming!"

After finding her some of Kate's clothes and bringing her upstairs, Bobby realized Wacka was hungry. He gave her normal foods—bits of grass trimmed from the side of the pond, a handful of sunflower seeds, and a few scraps of bread. She spat out the grass and seeds before shovelling the bread into her mouth.

"Y-Y-Y," she said, struggling to turn sounds into words. "YUM!"

"More bread?" asked Bobby.

"M-M-MORE B-BREAD," she stammered, as if the words were sticking in her mouth.

"Hey, you're learning to talk!" he said. "Great job, Wacka!"

"G-GREAT JOB, WACKA," said Wacka slowly. "MORE BREAD."

Wacka inhaled a few more slices of bread before finishing half the fruit in the bowl on the table. After she devoured her third apple—core included—Bobby set a plate in front of her.

"BREAD," said Wacka. "MORE BREAD."

"Not just bread," said Bobby, lifting the lid on her sandwich to reveal layers of meat, cheese, lettuce, and tomato. "This is a sandwich. *Sandwich*."

"SAND-WICH," she repeated. "BOB-BEE MAKE SAND-WICH F-F-FOR WACKA."

"Yup!" he said. "Try it."

Wacka lifted the sandwich to her mouth and took a bite. Her eyes rolled with pleasure as she savoured a big, sloppy mouthful.

"SAAAWHOOSH," she said between chomps.

Bobby laughed. "Don't talk with your mouth full."

Wacka ate the rest of her sandwich in silent rapture, slowly testing and tasting all the delights of bread, meat, vegetable, and sauce. After her last bite, she picked at the crumbs of bread left on her plate, apparently satisfied at last.

"What's next, Wacka?" asked Bobby.

"MORE SANDWICH!" she exclaimed.

"BONUS LEVEL!" yelled Wacka, hours later. "TAKE THAT, ALIEN SCUM!"

Wacka sat in the dark living room, her face illuminated by the glowing screen of the television. She gripped a video game controller in her hands as her character onscreen shot death rays into oncoming waves of alien attack fighters. Her right hand released the controller just long enough to dip into an empty plastic bowl sitting beside her.

"BOB-BEE!" she said. "MORE CHIPS, PLEASE."

Bobby stuck his face into the living room. "You're done the whole bag already?" he said, holding a tea towel and a wet plate in his hands.

"MORE CHIPS, BOB-BEE!" she repeated. "PLEASE?"

He sighed and turned back to the kitchen. "All right."

After Wacka had polished off two sandwiches, Bobby wondered what they should do next. His mind jumped to the activity he'd be most interested in: video games. For the last several hours, Wacka had been glued to the TV while he slaved in the kitchen preparing and cleaning up her snacks. It was, frankly, almost exactly like taking care of an eleven-year-old boy.

Bobby opened the snack cupboard and found it empty. "Bad news," he called to Wacka. "No more chips."

"NO MORE CHIPS?" said Wacka. "BOB-BEE?"

"Sorry," he said, walking into the living room. "Hey, let's shut that off. Why don't you come outside and stretch your legs? Maybe we can find Katie."

Wacka dropped the controller and jumped up. "F-F-FIND KATE! WACKA FIND KATIE!"

She rushed past Bobby, crossed through the kitchen, and smashed face-first into the outside door.

"OWW," she cried, her hand rubbing her nose. She slapped her other hand against the closed door. "LET WACKA OUT!" she insisted, pounding at the door. "LET WACKA OUT!"

"Hold on, hold on," soothed Bobby. He reached for the handle and turned it gently. The door swung open. "See? You have to turn the knob."

They walked into the cool darkness of the backyard. Crickets chirped in the long grass. The early fall air was refreshing. Dawn wasn't far away.

Bobby looked at Wacka. He just now noticed she'd put on her T-shirt backwards. She shivered in the cold and wrapped her arms around herself.

"Here," he said, zipping off his hooded sweatshirt and handing it to her. "You might need this."

She struggled with sliding her arms into the sleeves. "OW," she said. She clutched a spot on her arm.

"Is that where Marcus bit you?" asked Bobby.

Wacka nodded. It looked as if the memory hurt as much as the wound.

She gingerly pulled her arms through the sleeves of Kate's sweater. The zipper was a mystery to her, so Bobby helped her zip it closed. It reminded him of when his mum used to do the same for him, when he was little.

"COLD A BIT," she said, still shivering. "THANK YOU, BOB-BEE." She looked around. The night was still. "WACKA FIND KATIE NOW?"

"Sure. We can find Katie now."

Wacka inhaled deeply, filling her lungs to the bursting point, and released a loud and powerful scream:

"KAAAAAAAAAAAAAAAATIEEEEEE! WACKA FIND KAAAAAAAAATIEEEEEE!"

Bobby waved his hands in front of her mouth before she could scream again. "No, no!" he said. "Shhhhhhh! We have to be super quiet. Other humans might hear us."

"OTHER HOOMANS?"

"Yes, and they might not be nice to Wacka and Katie."

"NOT NICE TO WACKA?"

"No, so shhhhhhhhh," said Bobby, putting his finger to his lips.

Wacka mimicked this posture. "SSSSS," she said.

"Close enough," said Bobby.

They walked along the hedgerow toward the forest. The glowing light in the east was getting brighter.

"We'll look in the forest first," said Bobby. "Remember, we need to be very quiet."

"WACKA VERY QUIET," she said. "SSSSS."

"Wait," said Bobby, a few steps later. He held up his hand, motioning her to stop. "What's that sound?"

They stood in silence, listening. A faint whistle trilled in the distance, followed by a rhythmic sound like the beating wings of a duck.

"KATIE!" whispered Wacka, grabbing Bobby's arm. "WACKA HEAR KATIE!"

Kate flew at top speed toward Bobby, ready to scold him for the racket she'd heard moments ago. She landed at his feet and began to yell at him with quacks.

Kate had hardly begun her lecture when she was scooped up by the eager hands of Wacka.

"KATIE!" she said, overcome with emotion. "WACKA HOOMAN! WACKA HOOOOOMAN!"

Kate couldn't figure out who this strange girl was, or why she was shouting what sounded like nonsense in her face.

"KATIE!" said Wacka, holding the duck close to her mouth. She spoke slowly and seriously. "ME! WACKA! WACKA HOOMAN! BOB-BEE MAKE WACKA SAND-WICH!"

Kate understood just as the first rays of sunshine burst over the horizon.

"Wacka?" quacked Kate. "Wacka!"

Bobby watched as the sun bathed the duck and the girl with golden light. Their features seemed to melt as each began to transform. Wacka dropped Kate to the ground as she became smaller and covered in feathers. Kate's feathers withdrew into her skin as she grew larger. When it was all done, the girl and the duck standing in the dawn light had been replaced by a duck and a girl.

Bobby stood back. "Okay, that was cool," he said.

# CHAPTER FOURTEEN

"UGH," SAID BOBBY. HIS RUBBER BOOTS SQUELCHED in the mud. A cloud of mosquitoes swarmed around his face and neck. "Remind me again why we're in this swamp?"

"It's not a swamp," said his sister, three steps ahead. "Swamps are deeper and usually have trees. This," she said, sweeping her hand at the long grasses and cattails growing in the shallow water, "is a marsh."

"Okay, remind me again why we're in this *marsh*, then," said Bobby.

"We need cheese root," she said, not looking back.

"Right. Cheese root." He swatted a mosquito on his neck. "Remind me what that is again?"

Kate sighed. She pulled her knapsack from her back and slid out an old, yellow book. She opened it to a page marked with a slip of paper.

"'Cheese' is the folk name for a plant called swamp rose mallow," she said, pointing to the illustration of a large flower. "The Cure for Werewolf calls for the ground-up root of one of these. If we're going to make it, I'm going to need it."

"Right," said Bobby. He took the book and examined the page. "Remind me again why we're doing that?"

"At first, I just kinda wanted to see if the cure even worked," said Kate. "Now I think it would be cool to take a month off of being a duck to spend some time with Wacka when she's human." She smiled at the duck paddling in the shallow water beside her. "Right, Wacka?"

"Wacka," said Wacka proudly.

"Right," said Bobby, tucking the book under his arm. "I still don't really get why Wacka turned into a girl."

Kate lifted a pair of binoculars to her eyes and scanned the east bank of the marsh. "Marcus bit her. Usually, a werewolf bite turns a person into a werewolf. I guess, in this case, it turned Wacka into, like, a reverse wereduck."

Bobby scratched his head. "Hear that, Wacka?" he said, looking back. "You're a *reverse* wereduck."

"Wacka," said Wacka.

Kate lowered the binoculars and pointed. "I'm going to go over to the east bank," she said. "Why don't you keep looking along here?"

"Sure," he said. "Can I keep the book? I need to know what I'm looking for."

"Okay, but be careful," said Kate, handing it over. "That's the only copy. Marty The Librarian would flip if anything happened to it."

Kate strode through ankle-deep water, past lily pads and long grass. The cattails on the bank grew from a thick mat of entangled roots floating on the surface of the water. The book called this an ideal spot to find swamp rose mallow.

She picked her way through the water, careful to stay in the shallows. Her boots slurped in the mud as she worked along the edge of the cattail mat, searching among the long stems for a bright pink flower.

Kate had been searching this side of the marsh for several minutes before she realized she was alone. "Bobby," she called. "Do you have Wacka over there with you?"

"Nope," he yelled back. "I thought you had her." He grabbed at a small tuft of grass and pulled himself up the bank. Kate saw the old yellow book tucked into the back of his pants.

"Be careful!" she called to her brother before continuing her search. "Wacka! Where did you go?"

Kate heard a faint quack a short distance away. The duck must have paddled around a curve in the bank and was just out of Kate's eyesight.

"Coming!" yelled Kate.

Water and mud pulled at every step, slowing Kate's progress. "I'm on my way!" she called. She found the little duck swimming in frantic circles at the edge of the cattails.

"What is it, Wacka?" said Kate. "What's wrong?"

Kate gasped as she caught sight of the pink flower. The large blossom—light pink on the outside, fuchsia on the inside—looked just like the illustration in Muriel Tuttle's book.

"You found it!" said Kate. "You're a genius!"

Wacka closed her eyes and quacked proudly.

Kate dug a hand trowel from her backpack and attempted to dig the root from the marsh mat. She thought it would slide easily from the wet ground, but the finger-like roots of the plants around it held it fast in their grip. She sliced through them with her trowel, slowly freeing the mallow from the ground.

"Got it!" she said, holding her prize aloft like a sword. A long white root, thin like a carrot, dangled at the bottom of the plant. "Bobby, look! I got it!"

"All right!" he yelled. "Let me see!"

Bobby slid down the far bank, but missed his footing when his boots hit the mud. He swayed for a moment, flailing his arms for balance, and toppled head-first into the water.

"Bobby, no!" screamed Kate. She dashed across the marsh.

Water and mud dripped from Bobby's face as he pulled himself up. He wiped a layer of muck from his face. "Yuck," he said, spitting out a mouthful of water.

"Oh, no! Bobby!" cried Kate, rushing to his side. "No, no, no!"

"It's okay," he said, sitting up. "I'm all right."

"Not *you*!" she yelled. "This!"

Kate reached into the water and pulled out the old yellow book. Even after just a few seconds in the marsh, its cover was swollen with water. Its pages were covered in muck.

"Oh god, oh god," she said as she flipped pages. What little of the original ink that had remained was smeared beyond all legibility. "Bobby! It's ruined!"

"I'm sorry," he said. "But that was the last ingredi-ent, right? We won't need the book for anything else."

Kate whipped the recipe card out of her pocket and read it over. "*Second* last ingredient," said Kate. "I still need something called Kronos's blood. And without this book," she said, holding it like a club and whacking Bobby with every word, "I'll. Have. No. Idea. What. That. Is."

She sighed and slumped onto the ground at the water's edge. "And Marty is going to kill me," she said, thinking of the librarian. "It's his favourite book in the whole world."

"What are you going to do?" asked Bobby.

Kate thought. "I gotta tell him. He'd be even more upset if he thought I just stole it."

"What about the cure?" he asked.

"What about it?" said Kate. "Unless we have some other way of figuring out what Kronos's blood is, there's no use in even trying."

# CHAPTER FIFTEEN

KATE STOOD IN THE ENTRANCE OF THE LIBRARY, wondering whether she had the courage to do this. Confessing to Marty that she had ruined the book would destroy him. It would be so much easier to walk away and never show her face here again.

Kate sighed. No, that would be wrong. She closed her eyes and took a deep breath.

Marty sat at his desk, copying information into his ledger. Kate approached quietly and stood before him. He looked so peaceful, so focused; Kate almost didn't have the heart to disturb him. When he didn't look up at her, she cleared her throat. Marty kept scratching away at his ledger with a pencil.

Kate looked around. She really didn't want to bug him when he was so deep into his work. She cleared her throat again, a little louder.

Marty kept writing. He turned a page in the ledger

and started a new column.

"Um," said Kate softly, bouncing slightly on her heels, "Marty?"

Marty's pencil was flying across the page. He sat hunched so far over his work, his nose nearly touched the page.

"Marty," said Kate, full-voiced.

No response.

"MARTY?" she shouted.

Nothing.

Kate stepped forward. Short of driving a truck through the library, she wondered if there was any way to get this man's attention.

"EXCUSE ME," she said, placing her hand on the ledger in front of him.

Marty leaped screaming from his seat, knocking over the plant beside him.

Kate was so startled by his response that she, too, began to scream. She jumped back, knocking into a small library cart. The cart toppled over, spilling dozens of books on the floor.

"Aaaaaaaagh!" screamed Marty, looking back and forth from the books to Kate.

"Aaaaaaaagh! Sorry! So sorry!" screamed Kate. She reached across Marty's desk to pick up the overturned plant and accidentally bumped a glass of water, spilling it all over the open ledger.

"Aaaaaaaagh!" screamed Marty.

"Sorry! Aaaaaaaagh!" screamed Kate.

"Aaaaaaaagh!" screamed Marty. "Aaaaaaaagh," he said again, a little quieter. "Agh," he said again, his enthusiasm for screaming apparently fading.

Kate and the librarian stood looking at each other for a long moment, both breathing heavily.

"So," panted Marty, "Kate. Can I, um, help you with something?" His glasses hung around his neck from a thin, black cord. He polished one of the lenses with a tissue and put them on.

Kate disappeared and returned seconds later from the bathroom with a bunch of paper towels. "I'm really sorry, Marty," she said, sopping up the mess.

Marty broke into a nervous smile. "It's fine," he said, taking the paper towels. "I guess I got a bit, uh, absorbed in my work there."

Kate smiled back. Marty was such a nice, lovable guy. She felt horrible that she was about to break his heart.

"Marty," she said. "I'm afraid I have something I have to...show you."

"Oh, it can't be *that* bad, Kate," said Marty, drying the last of the spilled water from his desk.

There was nothing else left to do. Kate dug into her backpack and withdrew *Local Flora*, the volume Marty prized most in the whole library collection. It was a dirty, twisted mess.

Marty's hand touched his mouth. He squeaked and reached for the book.

"I'm so sorry," said Kate, handing it over. "I know it's very special to you and I—"

Marty's mouth opened to speak, but no sound came out. He turned the book over in his hands, looking for evidence that some of its contents had survived. He flipped through the pages. Not a word was legible.

"How—"

"I was using it to identify plants in Hillman Marsh," said Kate. She paused for a second, not wanting to blame her brother for dropping Marty's precious book in the mucky pond water. *Local Flora* was, ultimately, her responsibility and she had let him down. "It just slipped from my hands and...oh, Marty. I'm so sorry."

Marty collapsed onto his chair, overcome with emotion. He carefully closed the book and hugged it close to his chest.

"My...my *baby*," he squeaked.

"I know."

"Ruined."

"I'm so sorry."

Marty sighed. "It's...it's okay," he said, smiling bravely. "At least...you were using it the way Muriel Tuttle intended."

Kate felt horrible. She mustered a small smile. Marty's attempt at sympathy only made her feel worse.

"I'm really, really sorry," she said again. "I wish there was something I could do."

Marty looked up. "I know you do," he said. "Thank you, Kate. Why don't you go see John at the microfilm station while I, um, finish cleaning up around here."

Marty ran his hands along the canvas cover of the ruined book. He appeared to be trying to revive it with his fingers.

"Right," said Kate. "Okay." She surveyed the mess she'd made. "I can help—" she stammered, picking up a few books from the toppled cart.

"No, no," said Marty. "You've done enough."

Marty continued to cradle the old yellow book as Kate crept away. She found John at a desk in the back of the library, his face illuminated by a large projector screen. He was scrolling through what looked like images of an old newspaper.

"John," said Kate, touching his shoulder.

He was so engrossed in his reading, he jumped at her touch.

"What is *with* you guys?" she said. "Am I *that* sneaky?"

"Sorry, what?" asked John. His eyes were wide. His breathing was quick.

"Hey, are you all right?" asked Kate.

"I'm fine." John turned back to the screen. "But take a look at this." He paused dramatically. "Kate, I think I just found my mom."

# CHAPTER SIXTEEN

"*WHAT*?" GASPED KATE, TOTALLY THUNDER-struck. "I thought you said your mom was dead."

"That's the thing," John said. "My dad always said she died in a fire when I was a baby." He turned back to the microfilm viewer and scrolled through a series of articles. "I've been looking through old newspapers for stories about the fire for weeks." He gestured toward a stack of boxes. "My dad said I was born in Minnesota, so I started looking in their papers. Nothing. So I started looking in the papers from Wisconsin and South Dakota. Nothing. Marty has been awesome, getting microfilm records for papers all over the States, but there was nothing. So then I started looking in some Canadian papers. Look what I found."

He stopped scrolling and zoomed in on a headline: *"A WOLF STOLE MY BABY!" CLAIMS MOTHER*.

"This story is about a lady who says a wolf showed up one night and stole her baby from his bassinet," said

John. "Neither the baby—or the baby's father—was ever seen again. The police didn't buy the wolf story. Called it a kidnapping and a hysterical mother."

"Creepy," said Kate.

"And," said John, scrolling down, "check out this photo of the dad."

The black-and-white image showed a man with feathered hair and a bad eighties moustache, but there was no mistaking him. It was definitely John's father, Marcus.

"Holy crap," gasped Kate. "So, where is this? Where did it happen?"

"That's where it gets even weirder," continued John. "It was in New Brunswick. Some place called Boundary Creek."

"But that's just a few hours from where Bobby and I grew up!"

"I know. We were *that* close to my mom the whole time and I didn't even know."

Kate stared at the photo of Marcus, letting the details of the story sink in. "So what do we do now?" she asked.

"I know what I *want* to do," said John, turning to face her. "But first I gotta know. Are we friends again or what? I have a hard time keeping track."

Kate blushed. She nodded. "I'm sorry. I've been kind of silly."

John flashed a crooked grin. "I haven't really made it that easy, either. Buds?"

Kate smiled back. "Buds."

"Good," said John. "So here's the plan: I want to go see my mom. And I want you to come with me."

"Whoa, what do *I* have to do with any of this?"

"It's just," started John, looking down, "I don't want to do this alone."

Kate sat quietly looking at him. She didn't know what to say.

"Please?" he pleaded. "When we're actually speaking to each other, we make a pretty good team. Will you come?"

Kate swallowed hard. "Yeah," she said, surprising herself with how quickly she made the decision. She held his gaze for a few seconds.

"Great," he said. His eyes twinkled with mischief. He spun in his seat to face a laptop beside the microfilm station. "I already booked us two train tickets to Moncton. We leave a week from Tuesday."

"Wait, you *already* bought tickets?"

"Yup."

"You just assumed I would say yes?"

John beamed. "I *hoped* you would," he said. "I can be pretty persuasive." He fluttered his eyelashes.

Kate snorted a laugh. "Okay. How'd you even buy the tickets? You can't have made *that* much money picking tomatoes."

He shrugged. "Credit card."

"You have a credit card?"

"No." He reached into his pants pocket and pulled out a plastic card. "But our pal Dirt Bag does."

Kate yanked the card from his hand and stared at the name. Sure enough, it was Dirk Bragg—the reporter for *Really Real News* they'd dodged a few months earlier.

"How'd you get this?" she demanded.

John snatched it back. "Swiped it from his bedside table when we broke into his motel room last summer. Dad taught me to keep my eyes open for stuff like that."

"To be a thief?"

"Pfffft," he scoffed. "Cry me a river about Dirt Bag. That guy owes us."

"And you're not worried he'll notice a couple of train tickets showing up on his bill?"

"Dirt Bag might be good at some things, but taking care of himself ain't one of them," said John. "It's a miracle he puts pants on before he leaves the house most days. Plus, it won't show up on his bill until next month. By that time, we'll be long gone." He turned back to the laptop. "I booked the tickets online. We leave on the third. Thirty hours on the train."

"The third?" she asked.

"Yeah. Something wrong?"

"The third is the night of the full moon, genius. You'd think a werewolf would be better at keeping track of that."

"Oh, crap." He clicked back from the electronic receipt on the screen to the bookings page. "*Crap.*"

"What?"

"The tickets are non-refundable. I could buy us new ones, but that'll probably alert his credit card company that something is up. We go the third or we don't go at all." John slumped in his chair. He drummed his fingers on the desk and muttered to himself. After a moment, he perked up. "Unless...."

"Unless what?" asked Kate.

"Unless we take a night off of being a wolf and duck. How are you doing with that cure?"

Kate scowled. "I never told you about that."

John grinned.

"Bobby told?"

He shrugged.

"I'm going to kill him. Anyway. It's going lousy," said Kate. She explained about the ruined book and the missing ingredient. "Something called Kronos's blood," she said. "Whatever *that* is. Without the book, we're sunk."

Kate was just finishing her story when Marty rushed up from the front of the library. His eyes were wild with excitement. He carried the ruined copy of *Local Flora* in one hand and waved an open phone book over his head with the other.

"Kate!" he practically shouted. Every last bit of sadness seemed to have drained from of him. "Great news!"

"What is it?" she asked.

"Y'know how you said you wished there was something you could do about the book?" he said. "Well there *is*. I always figured Muriel Tuttle died *years* ago, but she seems to have the gift of longevity."

He thrust the phone book in front of her. It was open to the T section.

"Muriel Tuttle lives at 574 Concession C," announced Marty with a smile. He handed her *Local Flora*. "And you can go there yourself, on behalf of the library, to let her know *you* destroyed her precious, precious gift to the literary world with your utter disregard and carelessness. Isn't that *great*?"

Marty beamed as though he couldn't dream of a better opportunity. Kate and John stared at each other, each thinking the same thing. Maybe Muriel Tuttle could help them figure out what Kronos's blood was, and where to find it. And she just happened to live down the road from Aunt Bea.

"'Great' is the exact word I'd use, Marty," said Kate, sliding the ruined yellow book back into her pack.

# CHAPTER SEVENTEEN

THE PHONE WAS RINGING.

Dirk lay face down on his couch. A line of drool spilled from his open mouth. He closed his eyes tighter and wished whoever was calling would just hang up.

The phone kept ringing.

Dirk opened an eye. In any normal household, the call would have been picked up by voicemail by now. Dirk, however, had a deep distrust of voicemail, a service he had long believed was part of a government conspiracy to gather details on the lives of private citizens.

The details of this particular private citizen had recently become rather complicated. Dirk had been up late the night before recording his first country and western album for B&M Records. He'd written some songs for the record himself, including a ballad about the solitary life of a tabloid journalist and an upbeat number about the joys of a perfect banana. But the record company had also insisted that he record the song he'd humiliated himself with on national TV. The song he'd recently begun to loathe.

*"My wheels belong to the road…but my heart belongs to you!"*

It was a sore spot with Dirk. In the weeks since the wereduck story hit the news, he had certainly become successful. Famous, even. But as time wore on, it was becoming clear to Dirk that he wasn't famous for his journalism. Dirk was famous for being a fool. People didn't like Dirk for Dirk. They liked Dirk because they thought he was playing a character: a parody of a country music–singing tabloid reporter.

If only he could prove to them he was the real thing. If only he could prove his wereduck story was true.

The phone was still ringing. Dirk rolled himself off the couch and onto the floor. His fall was cushioned by an ankle-deep pile of dirty laundry and discarded newspapers. He reached out and grabbed the phone on the coffee table.

"Hello?"

"Hello, Mr. Bragg?" said a cheery voice. "This is Gina calling from Via Rail."

"Okay," said Dirk. He closed his eyes and considered hanging up.

"Mr. Bragg, I am just following up on your recent online booking with us: two coach-class tickets from Leamington, Ontario, to Moncton, New Brunswick. Can you please confirm the details of your trip are correct?"

Dirk sat up. He had definitely *not* booked tickets to go anywhere, but the words "New Brunswick" jolted him to attention. That was where his adventure with the wereduck had taken place more than a month ago.

"Well, it doesn't ring a bell, but I book a lot of trips for my work. Can you remind me of the details?"

"Sure, Mr. Bragg," said Gina. Her cheerful smile sparkled across the phone lines. "These tickets were booked online yesterday using your credit card. Two tickets, leaving Leamington, Ontario, next Tuesday, the third. That is an overnight trip, with stopovers in Toronto and Montreal."

"Right," said Dirk. He was half-listening while shuffling through the cards in his wallet, looking for his credit card. It was gone. "And can you tell me the names on the tickets?"

"I sure can, Mr. Bragg," sang Gina. "They're booked in the names of John DeWolf and Kate Duckenstein."

"*DeWolf* and *Duckenstein*?" repeated Dirk. His lips curled into a smirk. These kids were good, but they were sloppy. "Ah, yes. I remember now. My niece and nephew. Yes, of course I booked those tickets."

"Well, that is a relief, Mr. Bragg," said Gina. "There were enough suspicious details in the transaction that we thought we would confirm with you. Sorry to bother."

"Oh, it's not a bother at all," said Dirk, his mind devising a plan. "In fact, while I've got you on the phone, can you book me one more ticket?"

"Of course, Mr. Bragg. Where would you like to go?"

"I'd like to give my niece and nephew a little surprise," said Dirk. "You say there's a stopover in Montreal?"

"That's right, Mr. Bragg. The train arrives in Montreal at about seven-thirty in the evening and leaves again just after eight."

"Excellent. Book me on that one, please." He smiled with grim satisfaction. "I can't wait to see their faces when they see Uncle Dirk climb aboard their train."

# CHAPTER EIGHTEEN

"I STILL DON'T UNDERSTAND WHY I HAVE TO WEAR this dumb tie," said Bobby. He pouted as he walked with Kate and John up the tree-lined driveway of 574 Concession C—Muriel Tuttle's house.

"Because we're dropping in on an old lady," said John. "Old ladies like it when little boys wear ties."

Bobby tugged at the red and blue-striped fabric around his neck. "I hate this thing. I don't need to be here. You guys won't even let me go on your dumb train trip."

"Let's not forget it was your graceful antics that ruined the book in the first place," said Kate. "We need this lady to tell us what Kronos's blood is so we can finish the cure."

"And remember to speak loudly," interrupted John. "She's likely deaf as a post."

Bobby grumbled. The three approached the front steps to the white, wood-framed farmhouse.

"I hope she likes raisin cookies," said Kate nervously, eyeing the plate in her hands. "I still think we should have made chocolate chip. Most reasonable people hate raisins."

"Old ladies like raisins," replied John.

"You sure seem to know a lot about old ladies," said Kate. She knocked on the front door.

"Shut up," muttered John a split second before the door opened. An older woman with white hair and a black dress stood in the doorway.

"Can I help you?" she said with a quiet voice.

"Hello," said Kate politely. "We live just down the way. We were hoping to see Ms. Muriel Tuttle."

The woman looked at each of them with sad eyes. "Do you know my aunt Muriel? Are you friends?"

"Well, not exactly," said John. "We're neighbours."

"We brought cookies," said Kate, holding up the plate.

"How very kind of you," said the woman. "Yes, of course you may see her. Please, do come in."

She stepped aside to allow the kids to enter. The door gave a soft *click* as it shut behind them. Kate couldn't believe how still and dry the air seemed around her—like no one had opened a window in years. The house was so quiet she could hear a clock ticking in another room. The walls were papered in deep tones of red and gold. The heavy wood trim around the doorways was stained dark brown. A long hallway ran to the back of the house. The doors on both sides were shut. She led them through the kitchen and into an adjoining dining room.

The woman stopped them in front of a set of old wooden doors. She clasped her hands in front of her.

"My name is Netty Tuttle," said the woman. "Aunt Muriel would be very pleased to know you'd come."

"Oh, we moved in a while ago and have been meaning to introduce ourselves," said John, turning to Kate. "Weren't we?"

"Oh yes," nodded Kate. She nudged Bobby.

"Right," he added. "For weeks."

"Isn't that nice?" said Netty with a weak smile. "I only wish you'd come sooner."

She slid open the doors to reveal an old-fashioned parlour. The drapes were drawn. The lid of the piano keyboard was shut. But the dominant feature of the room was most definitely the coffin. Inside lay the body of a wrinkled old woman, her hands folded across her chest.

Netty motioned at the box. "This," she said, "is my aunt Muriel."

# CHAPTER NINETEEN

"IT IS A LOVELY GESTURE THAT YOU'VE COME TO pay respect to my dear auntie," said Netty, her eyes locked on the body in the coffin. "She was a fairly solitary woman. A bit of a hermit, actually. But I think you would have liked her."

"Well," managed Kate, choking back a combination of feelings that included shock, revulsion, and utter disappointment, "I—um—we, uh, just wanted to, uh, show how *sorry* we were...."

"So sorry..." said John.

"...to hear that, uh, Ms. Tuttle had died," continued Kate. "It certainly is...disappointing. Right, Bobby?"

Her brother stood with his mouth wide open.

"Sorry," Kate said to Netty. "He's just so sad, as we all are."

"I understand, dear," consoled Netty. "I'll leave the three of you for a few minutes to pay your respects."

"Oh, you don't have to do that—" stammered Kate.

"Such a brave girl," said Netty, patting Kate's arm. "You go ahead and say goodbye in your own way." Netty gave her shoulder a meaningful squeeze before excusing herself from the parlour.

The three stood staring at the body of Muriel Tuttle.

"Oh," said Kate.

She couldn't take her eyes off the sunken and wrinkled features of the old woman in the box.

"Yup," said John.

"Oh," repeated Kate.

John sighed deeply. "Yup."

Kate turned to Bobby. He hadn't moved in the last minute and a half. His mouth hung wide open. Kate realized her brother had never seen a dead body before. "You okay?" she asked.

"DEAD," said Bobby, his eyes locked on Muriel.

She put a hand on his shoulder. The poor kid was probably upset.

"Now we'll never know," continued Bobby. He blinked and looked back and forth from Kate to John. "Now we'll never know…whether she liked raisins." He smiled.

John burst out laughing, then quickly clamped his hand over his mouth.

"This is serious, you guys," scolded Kate. "How are we going to figure out what this Kronos's blood stuff is if the only person who knows is *dead*?"

"Maybe this Netty lady knows something," offered John.

"No way. We can't bother her about this stuff. She's in mourning," said Kate.

"I'm not saying we put a spotlight on her and give her the fifth degree. I'm just saying—" John stopped talking as Netty re-entered the room.

"There now," said Netty. "Such a neighbourly gesture of you to come. And look how nice you look in that tie," she said, gesturing to Bobby. He blushed. "Why don't you come to the kitchen? I've put on some tea, and we can have some of those cookies you brought."

"Sure," said Kate, relieved by the opportunity to leave the creepy coffin room.

They followed Netty to the kitchen and sat at a round wooden table. Light streamed through the window above the sink, illuminating a row of blue glass bottles. Kate smiled; they reminded her of the jars in her bedroom. She liked the way the light refracted through the glass, dappling the counter and floor with specks of blue light. This room wasn't like the rest of the house. Netty poured each of the kids a cup of tea.

John reached for the pitcher of milk. "I really am sorry we didn't get a chance to meet your aunt, Ms. Tuttle," he said. "Such an interesting woman. What a life she led."

Netty chuffed. "That's nice of you to say. I dare say, most people around here didn't even know she existed."

"I wouldn't say that," said John. "We're big fans."

"*Fans?*" asked Netty.

"Of her book," said John. "We got it out of the library."

"Oh, her book. You know, most people thought my aunt was a little strange, and that book was a big part of it. My father—Muriel's brother—always said it was awful queer of a body to spend so much time mucking through field and stream in search of *weeds*. But I just thought the world of Aunt Muriel. There'll never be another like her. She taught me everything I know about local flora."

Kate and John shot each other a quick glance.

"Oh, really?" said Kate. "I'm surprised more people aren't fascinated."

"What a thrill to find someone who appreciates wild plants," exclaimed Netty.

"We just think her book is invaluable," said John. "Especially the folk names."

"Right," continued Kate. "Without it, we wouldn't have been able to tell a beggar's button from a cheese root."

Netty's eyes went wide. She rested her teacup in its saucer. "You had a need for those, did you?"

"Well, yes," said Kate, worrying perhaps she was overdoing it. "We were making an old family remedy. Unfortunately, we had a bit of a problem before we could get all the ingredients."

"What happened?" said Netty.

Kate slid her backpack from her shoulder and withdrew the sodden copy of *Local Flora*.

"We borrowed this from the library and...."

"Oh, my," said Netty, taking the book.

"It was all my fault," said Bobby, miserably. "We were looking for cheese root when I slipped and...."

"Oh, my," repeated Netty. She flipped through the book. "You didn't miss a page, did you?"

The room was quiet for a moment as Netty finished examining the book. She sighed and put it down.

"Well, what's done is done," she said. "Maybe I can still help you."

"You can?' said Kate.

"Well, I'm not Aunt Muriel, but I did spend the better part of seventy years following her around the woods."

"Do you know about Kronos's blood?" said John bluntly.

Netty levelled a gaze at him, suddenly serious. "I do," she said.

"What is it?" he pressed.

"This is a curious combination of ingredients you're talking about," said Netty. "Beggar's buttons. Cheese root. Kronos's blood. What did you say it was for?"

Kate shifted in her chair. "An old family remedy."

Netty paused a moment before answering. "There's no mystery about blood of Kronos," she said. "It's just the sap of a cedar tree. Aunt Muriel has some of her homemade cedar syrup in the fridge, if you need it. She took a tablespoon every morning. Good for the blood, she always said."

"Oh, that'd be great!" said Kate, looking relieved.

"And purple loosestrife?" asked Netty. "You found some of that, I suppose."

Kate blinked. "Yes."

"And silver nitrate?" pressed Netty. "That give you any trouble?"

Kate shot a nervous glance at John. "We found some in an old chemistry set."

Netty rattled off the remaining ingredients to the Cure for Werewolf. "Did you find them, too?"

"How do you know—"

Netty sat up straight and began to recite:

*"If the wolf you seek to calm,*
*Let this potion be your guide:*
*A shot of silver, a soothing balm;*
*Still the beast that lives inside."*

All three kids stared at her in disbelief.

"I can recognize the ingredients for A Cure for Werewolf a mile away," said Netty, delighting in the shock on their faces.

"Ms. Tuttle, are you a—" began John.

"No, no," she said, laughing. "Not me. But you don't spend a lifetime searching for ancient remedies without learning a thing or two about the mysteries of this world. Including werewolves." She shook her head. "Oh, if only Aunt Muriel were here. She would have loved to have met you."

"You aren't going to tell anyone, are you?" said Kate.

"Heavens, no," said Netty. "Why would I do a fool thing like that?"

She crossed the kitchen to the fridge and pulled out a pint jar. She poured a small amount of sticky syrup into a smaller jar and sealed it. "Now, be careful with this," she said, handing the jar to Kate.

"Why, is it dangerous?" asked Kate.

"Oh, no. It's just sticky as all get out. Impossible to clean out of your clothes and hair." Netty smiled.

"Ms. Tuttle, can I ask you something?" said John.

"Of course."

"This cure. Does it work?" he asked.

"I've never heard otherwise," she said. "Though I hope you never need it."

"Why's that?" asked Kate.

Netty looked thoughtful. "I'm not sure what makes a sparrow a sparrow or a human a human," she said, "but I do know that changing one's nature isn't something that should be taken lightly. It's some powerful mojo."

"*Mojo*?" said Kate. She raised an eyebrow.

Netty smiled. "One of Auntie Muriel's favourite words, actually. Nature. Power. Magic. Whatever you want to call it," she said. "Now, is there anything else you need?"

"This is more than we thought we'd find," said Kate. "Thank you. And I'm really sorry your aunt died. I would have liked to have known her."

"And she would have loved to have known you," said Netty. Her eyes brightened as she thought of something. "In fact...."

She dashed from the kitchen to the study. The kids followed.

"I think she'd want you to have this," said Netty, digging through a deep pile of papers and books. Somewhere near the bottom, she found a yellow, canvas-bound book, identical in every way to *Local Flora* before it was destroyed. "Aunt Muriel made a couple of copies of that book. This is the only one left that I know of." She handed it to Kate.

Kate beamed. "I know a librarian who is going to be very happy to get his hands on this!"

# CHAPTER TWENTY

"ARE YOU DONE CHOPPING THE BEGGAR'S BUT-tons?" asked Kate, stirring a steaming pot on the stove.

"Yeah, they're right here," said John.

He picked up the wooden cutting block from the kitchen counter and scraped a pile of finely chopped grey and purple flowers into the pot.

"What's next?" he said.

"I think just the sap and the silver nitrate, and we're done," she replied. She carefully poured the syrup into the pot. John offered her a test tube filled with white crystals.

"This is the part I don't like so much," said John. "I'm okay with drinking icky stuff you found in the ditch, but this stuff looks like bad news."

Kate took the test tube. "I looked it up online. Too much of it gives you something called *argyria*. It turns your skin and internal organs blue."

"Cool," said Bobby.

"But we don't need that much," she said, using a thin strip of wood to pull out two tiny grains of crystal. She dropped them into the pot.

"This stuff smells horrible," said John, pinching his nose. "And I thought it would look more, y'know, potion-y."

Kate frowned. The simmering brown mixture didn't look terribly appealing or magical. Bits of herbs floated on the surface.

"Maybe we should strain it?" she suggested.

John examined the faded recipe card. "Doesn't say anything here about straining."

"What about the shot of silver?" said Bobby, reading over John's shoulder.

"What do you mean?" said Kate. "That's the silver nitrate."

"Yeah, but the poem says a *shot* of silver," he said. "I wouldn't call two tiny pieces a shot."

Kate frowned. "But that's just the poem, right? A key ingredient. 'A shot of silver, a soothing balm; still the beast that lives inside.'"

"I can read," snapped Bobby. "I'm just saying, it's weird."

"Well," said Kate, feeling unsure. She turned to John. "He's right. This whole thing is weird. This entire plan relies on a potion that we haven't even tested."

"Don't worry about it," said John. "If it doesn't work, we'll go with my backup plan."

Kate and Bobby stared at him.

"Do you want to share it with us?" said Kate.

"Y-yes," he said tentatively. "When it's finished. But I'm sure this potion is going to work. Netty said it would."

"No, she said she didn't have a reason to believe it *wouldn't*," said Kate. "That's not the same thing."

"You worry too much," replied John.

"But what happens when we're on the train, the full moon comes out, and this stuff doesn't work?" she said.

"Then there will be a werewolf and a wild flapping duck on a train," said John with a smirk. "It'll be exciting for everybody."

"I don't think this is funny," said Kate.

"Neither do I, so relax," said John. "I promise we won't get on that train without a solid backup plan. My dad wouldn't let us go anywhere without a plan for getting out. I'll think of something."

"He taught you a lot, huh?" asked Kate, arching an eyebrow.

John leaned against the counter and crossed his arms. "A lot of stuff like this, yeah," he said.

"Do you miss him?"

John shrugged. "I dunno."

"But he's, like, your *dad*," said Bobby.

"A dad who abandoned me in the middle of nowhere with people he barely knew," said John, getting angry. "A dad who lied to me my whole life about my mum. If that's what a dad is, no thanks."

Kate and Bobby looked nervously at each other.

"Look, I'll come up with a backup plan. I promise," said John. He looked Kate in the eye. "I won't let you down."

# CHAPTER TWENTY-ONE

"BOBBY," WHISPERED KATE, SHAKING HIM GENTLY.
"Bobby, wake up. It's time."

Bobby opened his eyes. The room was still dark.
He looked at the clock. It was just after five in the
morning.

"It's too early," he groaned, his head collapsing on
his pillow.

"We gotta go, Bobby," whispered John, sitting at
the end of the bed.

"Okay, okay," said Bobby, tossing aside his blanket. "I'm up."

"Meet us outside in two minutes," said Kate. "We
need to get Wacka packed."

Bobby dressed quietly in the dark. He grabbed an
apple from the bowl on the kitchen table and let himself out the back door. In the faint light of the moon, he
could see Kate fixing the latch on a pet carrier.

"I hate to put you in there, Wacka," said Kate through the door of the carrier. "It's just for a little while. I promise."

John crouched beside her. "It'll be fine, Wacka," he said. "Thanks for doing this."

"Wacka."

"Do you think she can understand us when she's a duck?" asked Bobby.

"For sure," Kate assured him. "We came up with a system. One quack for yes. Two for no. Wacka, do you want a treat?"

"Wacka!" quacked the duck.

Kate slipped a few sunflower seeds into the carrier. "Now, do you think John's backup plan is reckless and a bit ridiculous?"

"Wacka," quacked Wacka, bobbing her head up and down.

"Good girl," laughed Kate, giving her another treat.

"Hey!" said John. "It's a great plan!"

"Wacka wacka."

"Well, who asked you, anyway?" teased John. "Listen, if the cure works, we won't even need the backup plan. But if we do, I know we can trust Wacka."

"Wacka."

"Great," said John. "The train leaves in less than an hour. We have just enough time to walk into town to the station. Let's go."

"So, what am I supposed to tell Mum and Dad?" asked Bobby as the train came into view, lumbering toward the small town station.

"You don't have to tell them anything," said Kate, hitching her backpack higher on her shoulders. She picked up Wacka's cage. "I explained everything in the note."

The noise of the train grew louder as the engine roared slowly past, pulling a line of passenger cars behind it. The train rolled to a stop. A porter climbed down from a car and opened a set of collapsible steps.

"All aboard!" he called.

"Did you tell them in the note where you're going?" asked Bobby.

"No, dingbat," said Kate. "I don't want anyone chasing after us. We'll be back before too long."

"Can you at least tell *me* where you're going?" asked Bobby.

Kate rolled her eyes. "You'd tell, for sure."

"No, I wouldn't!" he protested. "I'm good at secrets."

"Like my secret about the cure?" said Kate. "What, did you wait a whole day before you told John? Look, it's for the best. I'll tell you everything when we get back."

John tugged at Kate's arm. "We really need to move," he said. He turned to Bobby. "Take care, Bobby. See you in a few days."

"See you," said the younger boy.

Kate hugged her brother. "It'll be okay," she reassured him. Inside, she wondered if that was true. She'd felt so confident in the plan earlier, but now that they were about to actually step on the train, she wondered if they were just being reckless. But she couldn't let Bobby know she was feeling doubtful. "Please tell Mum and Dad not to worry."

"Okay," said Bobby. He hugged her back. "See you."

Kate and John walked toward the porter, who smiled as they climbed into the passenger car. Kate turned and waved at Bobby.

"Bye," she mouthed.

Bobby waved back. "Be careful," he shouted.

"I will," she said. She turned and walked into the train car.

# CHAPTER TWENTY-TWO

BOBBY'S FEET CRUNCHED THE GRAVEL DRIVEWAY as he walked back to Aunt Bea's house. It felt so weird knowing Kate and John were already miles away on the train and getting farther away with every passing moment. He hadn't thought it would make him feel this way. He felt so alone. He missed them. He wished he wasn't coming home to an empty house, but he knew his mum and Bea were at work, and his dad and grandmother were in town to run errands. He stepped through the back door into the kitchen.

A pair of hands grabbed him from behind. One wrapped around his mouth to muffle his screams. The other wrapped around his body so tightly he could hardly move.

"Quiet," hissed a voice from behind him. "Stop squirming."

Bobby thrashed against his attacker. He knew that voice: it was John's father, Marcus. Bobby wrenched his body back and forth, trying to free himself, but Marcus was too strong. He breathed deeply and choked back the tears that welled up behind his eyes.

"That's better," said Marcus, when Bobby had stopped struggling. "Let's be reasonable people." He pushed Bobby into a wooden chair at the kitchen table. "Now," said Marcus, crossing his arms, "where's my son?"

"I don't know," said Bobby. He thought quickly. "I haven't seen him since we left New Brunswick."

"Oh, no?" sneered Marcus. "So that's not his bag by the couch? That's not his shirt hanging on the clothesline? Try again. Where's John?"

Bobby looked at the ground. "I don't know," he said finally.

"Shall I *help* you remember?" said Marcus, looming tall above him.

Anger burned in Marcus's eyes. Bobby glanced around the kitchen. His gaze fell upon an envelope on the counter—the note from Kate to their parents. They must not have found it before they left. He looked quickly back at the ground to avoid revealing too much, but it was too late. Marcus followed his gaze.

"What's this?" said Marcus, picking up the envelope. Scrawled across the front in Kate's handwriting was: *Mum and Dad. Don't panic.*

"'Don't panic'?" read Marcus. "What would your parents have to panic about?" He tore open the envelope and pulled out the folded paper. "'Dear Mum and Dad,'" he recited. "'By the time you read this, John and

I will be miles away. Please don't try to follow us. John has discovered his mother is still alive.'" Marcus cursed under his breath before continuing. "'We know where she is. We're going to find her. We don't know what will happen after that. Please don't worry. We will contact you in a few days and will be home very soon. Love, Kate. P.S. Bobby doesn't know anything.'"

Marcus balled up the paper and shoved it into the front pocket of his pants. He paced the kitchen floor and ran his hands through his hair. A corner of the note hung from his pocket.

"When did they leave?" Marcus demanded.

Bobby was silent.

Marcus placed one hand on each of the armrests of Bobby's chair and put his face close to Bobby's. *"When did they leave?"*

Bobby winced. "Just now. Half an hour ago."

"How are they travelling?"

"T-train."

Marcus stood up and thought a moment. "Okay," he sighed. "Here's what we're going to do."

He crossed the kitchen and started yanking open drawers. On the third try, he found a roll of silver duct tape.

"Get up," he said to Bobby. "Put your hands behind your back."

Bobby paused for a moment. He wanted to be the kind of guy who could fight his way out of this situation. Even if he wasn't strong enough to overtake Marcus, maybe he could outrun him—find some slippery trick to get past him. But no. Marcus had every advantage: he was bigger, faster, and he was standing between Bobby and the only exit. If Bobby was going to get out of this without getting hurt, he'd have to go along with Marcus. For now.

Marcus wrapped Bobby's wrists with tape. "Put your feet together," he ordered, before wrapping Bobby's ankles. Bobby could see what was coming next. If there was any chance to get that note out of Marcus' pocket, it was coming.

Marcus slung the boy over his shoulder and marched toward the kitchen door. Bobby writhed back and forth. "Put me down!" he shouted. He aimed his foot at the corner of paper sticking out of Marcus's pocket. He worked at the paper until half of the balled-up letter was exposed.

"Quit thrashing," growled Marcus. He carried Bobby behind the shed where an old car sat. Marcus tossed him into the backseat. It was littered with dirty clothes and empty fast-food bags. Bobby kicked one more time at the paper hanging from Marcus's pocket and watched it fall to the ground.

"Now," began Marcus, "we're going on a little trip, you and me. Are you going to come quietly, or do I have to put a strip of tape across your mouth, too?"

"Don't. Please," said Bobby. "Just let me go. I won't say anything. I promise."

Marcus scoffed. "Too late for that." He slammed the back door and then let himself into the driver's seat. He started the car and began to drive.

In the back seat, tears streamed down Bobby's face. He was angry. He was terrified. His one tiny hope was that someone would find Kate's crumpled letter and figure out that something had gone seriously wrong.

# CHAPTER TWENTY-THREE

KATE AND JOHN WALKED DOWN THE CROWDED aisle of the train, trying to find a pair of seats together. The car was packed with grumpy-looking people in business suits. Some tapped away at laptops, others read newspapers or fiddled with their phones. None looked like they wanted to yield their seats to a couple of teenagers.

Near the back of the car, they found two seats across the aisle from each other. Kate squeezed herself into one with Wacka's cage on her lap. She smiled in greeting at the woman sitting next to her. The woman frowned and turned to stare out the window.

"Do you think the whole ride will be like this?" Kate asked John across the aisle, who sat beside a large, snoring man.

"Dunno," said John. "It'll be a long trip if it is."

They sat in uncomfortable silence for a few minutes before a man came down the aisle in a conductor's uniform. With his stiff cap and thin moustache, he looked as if he had stepped out of a railway car from the 1930s. He stopped in front of John and Kate and stood with his hands behind his back.

"You're my new passengers, yes?" he said.

Kate and John looked at each other. "Yes," answered Kate.

"Tickets, please," he said, extending a hand.

Kate dug her ticket from her backpack. John fished his from his pocket. The conductor snatched them up and stared at them long enough that Kate worried something was wrong.

"You're with us all the way to Moncton?"

"Yes," said John.

"It's a long trip."

John looked from Kate to the conductor. "Yup."

"And it's just the two of you, is that right?"

"Yes, just us," said Kate. The corner of Wacka's carrier dug into her knee. She readjusted herself in the cramped seat. "Will it be this crowded the whole way?"

The conductor looked up from the tickets. His eyes twinkled as he flashed Kate the smallest of grins.

"It *is* a bit stuffy in here," he said, ripping the ends off their tickets and handing the stubs back. He leaned forward. "Most of these people are business commuters on their way to Toronto. A troupe of clowns could burst in and they wouldn't notice a thing."

Kate and John smiled.

"Tell you what," said the conductor, "come with me."

Kate and John followed the conductor to the back of the car and through a door.

"We're not supposed to open the next car until we get past Toronto," said the conductor, leading them through the noisy space between cars and through another door, "but you've got a big trip ahead of you."

Besides being empty, this car was much more comfortable, with wider seats and space to spread out. The conductor led them to a set of four seats facing each other, two and two, across a table.

"I think this will be a bit nicer," he said, pushing Kate's bag into an overhead bin.

"Wacka," came a small quack from the pet carrier.

"And who have we here?"

Kate smiled. "This is Wacka. She's my pet duck."

The conductor stuck his finger into the grill of the cage door and stroked her beak. "I've worked on this line for twenty-six years," said the man. "I can honestly say, you, Wacka, are my first duck passenger. Welcome aboard."

"Thank you so much," said Kate. "This really is much better."

"We move a lot of people on this train, but I like to take special care of the folks who are in it for the long haul. So, settle in. You've about thirty hours to Moncton. If you need anything, just ask."

He smiled one last time and left.

"Wow," said Kate, smiling across the table at John. "This is...nice."

"Yeah," he said, looking out the window to watch telephone poles whiz past. "This really couldn't be going any better."

# CHAPTER TWENTY-FOUR

"QUIT CRYING," SAID MARCUS FROM THE DRIVER'S seat. "I mean it. Quit that."

Bobby lay in the back seat of the car. His ankles and wrists were sore from the tape. His face was wet with tears. He sniffed.

"I'm not going to hurt you," said Marcus. "Just stop crying, all right?"

"You already hurt me," said Bobby.

"I couldn't leave you there," said Marcus. "Just think of it as coming along for the ride. If everything goes fine, I'll let you go tomorrow, and it'll be like nothing happened."

Bobby lay in the back seat. It didn't feel like nothing was happening. He adjusted his weight to make himself more comfortable. A hard object was digging into his back. He scooted along the seat to grab whatever it was with his hand.

"None of this is my fault," Marcus protested from the front seat. Sometime in the last half hour, his tone had switched from angry to defensive. "*Your* family took *my* kid. And now he's gone off and run away with *your* sister. She probably put him up to it. And they'll find nothing but trouble if they get to that woman before I get to them."

Bobby said nothing. His hand was getting closer to the object jabbing into his back. If he could just get his fingers around it....

"And all this on a full-moon night," said Marcus, his anger rising. "What're they going to do when the sun goes down and they're stuck on a train? Did they think about that?" He looked at Bobby in the rear-view mirror. "Did they *think* of that?"

"Yes."

"Well, how are they going to get around that little inconvenience?"

"They have a...potion."

"Potion?" exclaimed Marcus. He kept glancing from the road to the rear-view mirror. "Cure for Werewolf? Is that what you're talking about?"

"Yeah, that's what it's called," said Bobby. His fingertips touched the object digging into his back. It was made of hard plastic.

"And they're planning to *drink* it?"

"Yes," said Bobby. His hand wrapped around the object. It was an old cellphone. He clutched it tightly.

"Just great," said Marcus sarcastically. "They might as well drink a bottle of ketchup, for all the good it'll do them." He scoffed and stared straight out the front window. "That stuff doesn't work," he said. "Not if you *drink* it."

Bobby explored the phone with his fingers, trying to get his bearings on the old numeric keypad. He rubbed the buttons with his thumb, trying to remember which numbers corresponded to which letters.

*Number 2 is ABC,* he thought. *Number 3 is DEF....*

He pressed the power button.

The phone beeped.

Bobby held perfectly still for several moments to make sure Marcus couldn't hear it over the sound of the highway. If he could do this quietly, it might be his only chance to let his parents know what had happened to him.

He pressed a button, beginning the most important text message he would ever send.

# CHAPTER TWENTY-FIVE

JOHN'S EYES WERE CLOSED. HIS BREATHING WAS slow and rhythmic. He had balled his sweater into a pillow and tucked it into the corner between his seat and the window. His hands lay folded on his lap. His mouth hung slightly open.

Kate tried very hard, but couldn't sleep. The train made a continuous *click-click, click-clack* as it rolled through the eastern Ontario countryside. They'd been riding for several hours now, including a stopover in Toronto around midday. Around her, Kate could hear the quiet chatter of some of the passengers they'd picked up along the way.

She opened her eyes and looked at John. He was drooling a bit. She smiled.

This boy was capable of making her feel so many things. She thought of this past summer when she had been so angry with him she couldn't even look at him. And then one evening—at a bowling alley of all places—she had realized she liked him. Like, *liked* him, liked him. And she was sure he liked her back. For those few minutes, it was the feeling she'd always imagined—knowing the person you love actually loves you back.

Until you find out he doesn't.

Living with him was such a roller coaster. Sometimes she resented him. Sometimes she adored him. He was so infuriating. He was so fun.

Kate sighed. She couldn't figure out what she felt for him.

The train blew a long blast of its horn as it crossed a rural highway. John stirred. He stretched and looked back at Kate with groggy eyes.

"What?"

Kate blushed. "You're drooling."

"Oh, god," he said, putting his hand to his mouth. "Sorry."

They sat quietly, watching trees and farmland rush past the window.

"Hey," he said. "Thanks for doing this. I know you didn't have to."

"It's okay."

"No, really," said John. "I know this isn't a small thing, going across the country like this. I really appreciate it."

"No, *really*," she said back. "It's okay. We're friends."

John smiled a sleepy smile and leaned back into his seat. "Best friends," he said. "I've never had a best friend before."

"Really?"

"We moved so much, I never got to know anybody." He rested his head back onto his sweater-pillow and closed his eyes. "I didn't want to do this alone. Thanks, Katie."

Kate wrapped her arms around herself. "No problem."

John had such an easy way about him, she'd always assumed he'd had lots of friends. It was hard to imagine him needing anyone, let alone her.

She balled her own sweater into a pillow and laid her head on it. She felt warm inside. She knew exactly how she felt for this boy.

"That's what best friends are for," she whispered, closing her eyes, finally ready for a rest.

# CHAPTER TWENTY-SIX

MARGE AND BRIAN WALKED CHATTING AND laughing into the house, each carrying a pair of grocery bags. Lisa met them at the kitchen door.

"Have you seen the kids?" she asked them.

"Nope," said Brian, setting his bags on the counter. "They're not here?"

"No, and I didn't see them this morning, either," said Lisa.

Marge frowned. "It's not like them to be gone for so long without telling us."

"What's the worry?" asked Brian. "I'm sure they'll be back soon."

Lisa scowled. "It's just—the house was a disaster when we got back. Chairs knocked over. Drawers left open. And the back door was wide open."

"That's odd," said Brian.

The door burst open and Bea walked in, reading a crumpled piece of paper. "You are not going to believe this," she said.

"Believe what?" said Lisa.

"Kate and John are off searching for his mom," she said, holding up the letter from Kate.

"Where'd you find that?" asked Brian, snatching it from her hands.

"Crumpled up in a ball out in the driveway."

"This is all very odd," said Marge. "Why wouldn't they leave it in the house where we'd find it?"

"And what about Bobby?" said Brian, finishing the letter. "'P.S. Bobby doesn't know anything,'" he read.

"Well then, where is he?" demanded Lisa. She grabbed the letter from her husband.

"It doesn't make sense," said Brian. "Whatever plan they made, it looks like it's already gone wrong."

"Okay," said Marge. "We're not doing any good working ourselves into hysterics. Brian, put the kettle on."

"But—" he began.

"But nothing," she cut him off. "I've yet to see the situation that couldn't be helped by a cup of tea."

Brian begrudgingly grabbed the kettle and filled it from the tap.

"Now," said Marge, taking control. "Let's start with what we know. The letter says Kate and John are on their way to his mother's house." She looked at each of them. "I thought she was dead."

"So did I," said Bea.

"Well, they must know something we don't," said Marge flatly. "Anyone have any idea where Marcus and John are from, originally?"

"I always assumed the States, but I never heard for sure," said Brian.

The whole group turned to Bea. She shrugged.

"Let's count that as an 'I don't know,'" said Marge. "So if the kids have somehow figured out in the last two months where she is, how did they do it?"

The group was silent. Lisa sat on a kitchen chair and crossed her arms.

"John's been at the library an awful lot," she said.

"Okay," said Marge. "What's he been doing there? He certainly hasn't been bringing home any books."

No one had an answer.

"I think that's where we start," decided Marge. "Bea, you come with me to the library. Lisa and Brian, stay here. Drink some tea. They may show up yet."

As Marge finished her sentence, Lisa's cellphone beeped in her pocket. She fished it out and read the screen.

"Brian!" she gasped. "Look!"

She handed him the phone.

"Oh my god," he said.

*Marcu S g0t me b0bbY 911*

# CHAPTER TWENTY-SEVEN

MARTY WHISTLED TO HIMSELF AND LOOKED AT the clock. Three minutes to six. In just a few minutes, he could close up the library, grab a quick bite, and be home in time to catch the latest episode of his favourite TV show, *K9 Runway All Stars*.

He closed the ledger in front of him and was about to switch off his desk lamp when the front door opened. Two women walked in.

"I'm sorry," he said, "we're closing in—"

"Oh, we'll just be a minute," said the older woman. Marge approached the counter and looked him in the eye. "My grandson, John, has been coming in here quite a bit. I was wondering if you know him."

"John?" said Marty, brightening. "Of course I know him. Lovely kid." He turned to Bea. "You must be...his mother?"

"Ah, no," she said, smiling. "I'm his...auntie."

"Well then," said Marty. "What can I help you with?"

"He's been working on a special project," began Marge. "For school. A research project."

"Okay," said Marty. "That explains all those hours at the microfilm station. I've been curious about what he was working on, but I didn't want to pry."

Bea and Marge looked at each other.

"Right," said Bea. "Well, before he hands it in to his teacher, he wants us to check some things over. There were some facts we wanted to make sure he got right."

"Okay," said Marty. "He went through dozens of spools of microfilm. Do you have any idea where you'd like to start? This is something that might take a bit of time." He eyed the clock.

"Oh, we'll just be a minute," said Marge again.

"When did you last see John, by the way?" asked Bea.

Marty scrunched his face. "Must be—gosh—a week? I miss him. He was here every day for so long. I was getting used to having him around. But one day he just stopped showing up."

"Right," said Marge. "I'd like to take a look at the last roll of film he was looking at. That's the one he said to check."

"No problem," said Marty, standing up from his desk. "Honestly, he left in such a rush that day, and no one—I mean no one—ever uses the microfilm station. I think it may even be still spooled up in the machine."

Marty led them to the back of the library. He flicked a switch on the microfilm station. The screen lit up with a giant newspaper headline.

*"A WOLF STOLE MY BABY!"* CLAIMS
*MOTHER.*

Bea gasped.

"Yes, that's the one," said Marge calmly. She
placed a reassuring hand on her daughter's arm. "Just
let me read that over quickly to confirm the details."

Marty yielded the seat to Marge. She read it carefully, jotting down a few notes, and stood up.

"That's everything we needed," she said. "You've
been so kind. Thank you so much, Mister...."

"Marty," he said, smiling and extending his hand.
"Please. Call me Marty."

"Well, thank you, Marty," said Marge, shaking his
hand.

Marge escorted her speechless daughter out of the
library. Once on the sidewalk, she whispered into Bea's
ear. "For the love of...they're on their way back to New
Brunswick. Marcus stole John right from his crib in a
place near Moncton called Boundary Creek."

"Then Marcus must be—" began Bea.

"—on his way to stop them," finished Marge.
"We'd better warn that woman before the big bad wolf
shows up at her door."

# CHAPTER TWENTY-EIGHT

KATE SQUEEZED OUT OF THE TINY BATHROOM AT the back of the train car. Somehow, that room seemed to get smaller and smaller the farther east they travelled. The smell wasn't improving either.

She half-swayed, half-walked up the narrow aisle in rhythm with the train. More than eight hours into their trip, she realized her body had become used to the *click-click, click-clack* of the rocking train.

"I'm going up to the snack car. You want anything?" Kate said to John when she arrived at their seats.

"Nah, I'm good," he answered, looking up from his book.

"You want to come with me? Stretch your legs?"

He put his feet up on the chair opposite him, put his hands behind his head, and let out a deep, contented sigh. "You mean, more than this?"

"Why is it that boys take up as much space as possible wherever they go?" said Kate, knocking his feet off the seat as she walked past.

To get to the snack car, Kate needed to navigate through four cars' worth of burly passengers, feet stuck into the walkway, and a two-year-old boy running up and down the aisle screaming "I'm an airplane! VROOOM! I'm an airplane! VROOOOM!"

In comparison with the sardine-packed passenger cars, the snack car was beyond spacious. Only a few tables and booths were scattered throughout. A family with small kids sat around one table in the midst of what appeared to be an intense game of crazy eights. A pair of older women played chess at another. The rest of the passengers were engrossed in a bad action movie playing loudly on a TV screen in the corner. Kate approached the concession stand, where a uniformed man sat leafing through a tabloid newspaper behind a row of chips and prepackaged sandwiches.

"Hi," he said, laying the newspaper face up on the counter in front of Kate. "What can I get you?"

"Uh," said Kate, staring at the front page of the newspaper. All thoughts of a snack had vanished. "I, uh…."

"A bag of chips, maybe?" suggested the man. "Something to drink?"

Kate was frozen.

"You okay?"

Kate blinked. She pointed at the newspaper. "How much for that?"

He picked it up. "This? Oh, this is mine. I'm all done with it if you want it."

Kate nodded, her eyes still fixed on the front page.

"You want something to eat as well?" he asked, handing over the paper.

"Chips," blurted Kate. "Barbecue."

"Great. That'll be two thirty-nine."

Kate dug into her pocket and laid a five-dollar bill on the counter. She walked away, clutching the paper to her chest.

"Hey, don't you want your change?" called the man.

Kate nearly breezed right past her seat when she returned, her face buried in the newspaper as she walked. John managed to flag her down.

"What's so interesting?" he asked, grabbing the bag of chips from her hands and tearing it open.

"Oh, just the *worst possible thing that could possibly ever happen*," said Kate, thrusting the magazine at him.

John turned the paper over. *NIGHT OF THE WEREDUCK*, screamed the full-page headline superimposed on an image of the full moon.

"Oh. My. Gosh."

"It gets worse," said Kate, yanking the paper from him and flipping through to the article. "Listen to this: 'Senior investigative reporter Dirk Bragg spent months in pursuit of an elusive and vicious band of werewolves living in secret in eastern Canada,'" read Kate. "'What he found was a story even more than it was quacked up to be.'"

"Ugh," groaned John.

"I know," agreed Kate, turning the page. "The whole thing is a bunch of lies about how we tried to kill him. It makes him come off like some kind of superhero."

"Idiot," said John.

"But look at this. He tells the story of how I turned into a duck. They hired a police sketch artist to draw a picture of me."

She turned the newspaper to reveal a sketch that looked remarkably like Kate.

John whistled. "Pretty good likeness, actually."

Kate looked at it again. "You think? I think he made my nose too big." She touched her face. "Anyway," she continued, slamming the paper on the table, "this is horrible."

"Horrible," repeated John, taking back the paper and leafing through its pages.

"Terrible!" said Kate.

"Terrible," said John mindlessly, turning a page.

"The absolute, most worstest-worst thing that could happen!" she said.

"I couldn't agree more," said John lazily. He flipped the page.

"Then *why* don't you seem THE LEAST BIT CONCERNED BY THIS?"

"Because look!" said John, showing her a headline. "*'PINEAPPLES ARE ALIEN BRAINS GROWING FROM THE GROUND!'*" He flipped a page. "And this: *'THIS BABY ATE A WHOLE GERMAN SHEPHERD!'*"

"Very funny," said Kate.

"Come on," said John. "Yeah, the story seems bad, but put it in context. Who is going to believe anything written in *Really Real News*?"

"I suppose," she said, grabbing the bag of chips John had left on the table. She crunched one and watched trees whiz by the window. "D'you think Dirt Bag is still out there looking for us?"

"I dunno. Maybe," said John. "He's the least of our troubles. He won't know about this until he sees the charges on his credit card bill next month. The chances of him finding us right now on a train speeding across Canada are about zero."

Kate sighed. "I guess you're right."

John's confidence made her feel a bit better, but she couldn't shake all her worries. This entire plan relied on a whole lot of things going right. If she'd learned anything in the last few months, it was that things rarely work out the way you expect them to.

# CHAPTER TWENTY-NINE

DIRK DRUMMED ON THE STEERING WHEEL OF HIS truck in time with the country song blaring from his radio. He'd been idling for nearly half an hour at the border crossing between the United States and Canada, just south of Montreal. There was just one car left in line in front of him. In just a few minutes, he'd be cleared through Canadian customs and on his way to the train station to ambush an unsuspecting werewolf and wereduck.

Dirk stopped mid–drum solo to prepare for the customs inspection. He leaned over and opened his glovebox. An avalanche of papers slid to the floor.

"Shoot," he hissed.

Dirk looked up and saw the driver of the car in front of him was handing paperwork to the border guard. He had just a minute or so before it was his turn.

Dirk pushed papers back and forth on the ground. The corner of a small blue booklet caught his eye.

"Bingo!" He picked up his passport and leaned back in his seat.

In front of him, the driver had stepped out of his vehicle and was being led by the border guard to the trunk of his car. The driver unlocked it and pulled out a grocery bag. The guard reached in and withdrew an orange.

*Shoot,* thought Dirk. *Am I not allowed to bring in fruit?*

He glanced around the inspection booth and saw a large sign reminding travellers to declare all produce in their vehicles.

He looked to the seat beside him. Three bunches of bananas sat piled in a heap, each in varying shades of ripeness. The bunch on the bottom was nearly black.

"Shoot!" he said out loud.

He looked at the floor of the passenger seat. Under the pile of papers from the glovebox, the floor was carpeted with banana peels.

The driver ahead of him handed the bag of oranges to the border guard, who tucked them inside the door of his customs booth. There didn't *seem* to be a problem—*But you never can tell with authority figures in mirrored sunglasses,* thought Dirk. The driver stepped back into his vehicle. The brake lights on his car flared red; Dirk realized it was almost his turn.

"Shoot," he said again. "Shoot, shoot, shoot."

He yanked a green shopping bag from between the seats and began to stuff it with bananas and peels. He needed to get rid of the evidence or he might be denied entry, or something much worse—everyone knew Canadian border guards belonged to a secret and ancient society bent on control of the global banking system through a sophisticated campaign of computer cracking, kidnapping, and confiscating small amounts of fruit from international travellers. Dirk leaned over to scrape slimy peels from the floor of the truck.

*Knock, knock, knock.*

Dirk jolted upright to find the border guard tapping on his window. Dirk flashed him a nervous smile and rolled down the glass.

"Care to pull your truck forward, sir?" said the guard. He had a generous moustache. His mirrored sunglasses glinted in the sun.

"Oh, uh," said Dirk, his face flushing red. "Yes. Sure. Of course. Sorry. Yes."

He put his truck in gear and pulled it up to the booth.

"Now," said the border guard flatly, "what was so distracting that you had to hold up the *entire* line of cars behind you?"

"Oh, uh," said Dirk, casting about, "I guess I was, uh—"

"What's in the bag, sir?" demanded the guard, eyeing the item sitting beside Dirk on the seat.

"Just some, heh, y'know...."

Dirk handed the bag of rotten peels and bananas through the window. Black juice dribbled from the bottom. The border guard winced at the smell.

"Bananas?" he said, holding the bag at arm's length. A puddle of juice began to gather at his feet.

"Bananas," repeated Dirk. He grinned weakly. He thought of the rumours he'd heard of the unsuspecting, fruit-carrying travellers who passed through the border and were never seen or heard from again.

"Well, shoot," said the border guard. He flung the bag into a nearby garbage bin. A slow smile spread across his face. "So many people freak out at the last minute because they've got a bit of fruit in the car. Don't worry about that."

Dirk sighed. "Oh, thank goodness."

"Though, that is disgusting," said the guard, motioning toward the garbage bin. His smile faded.

"I know," said Dirk.

"Like, *really* disgusting."

Dirk paused. "I'm sorry."

"Seriously," said the guard, reaching for a bottle of hand sanitizer. "That's the grossest thing I've seen come through here in a long time."

"I'm, uh—"

"But I can't deny you entry for being a disgusting human being," said the guard, rubbing sanitizer into his palms. He levelled his mirrored sunglasses at Dirk. "So, I'm going to need to see your passport."

Dirk handed it over.

"Dirk Bragg," slowly read the guard. "That sounds familiar." He looked back and forth between the passport photograph and Dirk. "You famous or something?"

"Not really."

"What do you do for a living?"

"I'm a journalist."

"Journalist? I swear I've seen your face before."

The guard swivelled to shout at the border guard working in the next lane.

"Hey, Bert! Bert! You ever hear of someone named Dirk Bragg? Was he on TV or something?"

The second guard looked up from his conversation

with another driver. "Dirk *Bragg*? He's the werewolf guy! From *America This Morning*!"

"Holy heck!" said the guard, turning back to Dirk. "You're the werewolf guy from the TV!"

"Oh. Uh—" stammered Dirk, smiling nervously.

"Man, that was hilarious," said the border guard. "You sure did pull a fast one on that old TV guy." He turned back to his co-worker. "Remember that song he sang, Bert? What was that again?"

Bert looked up. *"My wheels belong to the road!"* he began.

*"But my heart belongs to yoooooou!"* sang the two border guards together before breaking into laughter.

"So what are you up to now?" asked the guard, his cheeks red with laughter. "Another werewolf hunt?"

Dirk slumped in his seat and looked forward. "Something like that."

"Well, then," said the guard, handing back his passport. "I wish you luck."

"I'm free to go?"

"You are," said the guard. He leaned forward and winked. "Don't get bit by any werewolves now. HA HA HA HA HA!"

"Ha. I'll try." Dirk let out a long breath and put his truck into gear.

"Hold up, hold up," said the guard, stopping Dirk before he could pull away. He yanked off his sunglasses. His eyes narrowed. "I need just one more thing."

Dirk gulped. "What's that?"

The guard pulled his phone from his pocket.

"Mind if I take a selfie with you?"

# CHAPTER THIRTY

TALL LIGHT STANDARDS WHIZZED PAST BOBBY'S window—the kind that usually illuminate a major highway. He couldn't see what direction they were driving. He had no idea how far they'd driven. All he could tell was that for the first time in many hours, the car was slowing down.

"Where are we?" Bobby dared ask.

"Highway rest station," said Marcus. "I'm running out of gas. Time to find another ride."

"But once the sun goes down, won't you become a—"

"Quiet," interrupted Marcus. "I know what I'm doing."

Bobby felt the car manoeuvre off the highway. He could see the occasional treetop through the window. The car pulled to a stop. Marcus put the car in park and swivelled in his seat to look at Bobby.

"I'm going to be gone for two minutes, but I will be within earshot of the car the whole time. If you yell, I will hear you. Got me?"

Bobby nodded.

The driver's door slammed shut, leaving Bobby alone in the car. He thought of sending another text message to his parents. He fiddled with the phone behind his back, finding and pressing the power button. Nothing happened. The battery was dead.

Before he could mourn the loss of his last connection with home, the door beside him opened. Marcus leaned in and started ripping the duct tape off Bobby's wrists and ankles.

"Now," he said, yanking away the last bit of tape, "I've found us another ride. Before you even think about running away, consider: I'm bigger. I'm faster. I'm stronger. Understand?"

Bobby nodded. His arms and legs were so sore from being bound, he didn't know whether he could walk, let alone run.

"I understand."

"Good," said Marcus. His features relaxed. "This doesn't have to be difficult. I know it may be hard for you to understand, but I don't want to hurt you."

Bobby sat up and swung a tentative foot to the ground. A cramp gripped his thigh. He gasped.

"You okay?" said Marcus.

Bobby nodded. Marcus held out his hand. Bobby stared at it a moment before reaching out to grab hold. Marcus pulled him gently from the car.

"Stretch your legs a bit," he advised. "You'll be pretty stiff, I imagine."

Bobby attempted to take a step and nearly fell over. Pain stabbed the back of both his knees. His legs had been stuck in the same position for so long, they were almost too stiff to move.

"Ouch," said Marcus, wincing at the boy's pain. "Try stretching one at a time."

Bobby held onto the side of the car for support as he lunged forward to stretch first his left knee, then his right. He rubbed the back of his thigh to work out the knots.

"All right, we don't have much time," said Marcus, slinging a small pack over his shoulder. "Come on."

He led the boy across the parking lot to a row of idling semi-trucks. He stopped beside the cab of a red truck attached to a dirty white semi-trailer. A scruffy man with a brown ball cap nodded at them as they approached.

"Boundary Creek by dawn, right?" said Marcus in reply to the silent greeting.

"I've gotta be in Halifax by mid-morning, so that's on the way," said the man. "I don't see why you want to ride in the back, though. Plenty of room up front."

"Call it a bit of adventure for my son and me," said Marcus.

The driver nodded at Bobby. "Couple of modern-day hobos, is that it, boy? Kind of like riding the rails."

Bobby didn't know what to say. He looked down. Marcus nudged him.

"Yeah," said Bobby quietly. "Like riding the rails."

The driver shrugged. "Suit yourself then."

He climbed down from the cab and led them around to the back of the trailer. He lifted the latch on the door and pulled it open. "Hop in," he said.

The cargo bay contained showroom furniture. Box springs and mattresses filled the front of the truck. Tables and chairs were piled in the middle with a couple of soft-looking couches stacked right behind them. The driver grinned. "You'll be comfortable enough," he said. "Be glad I'm not hauling a load of pigs like last week."

Marcus climbed into the back of the truck and pulled Bobby up by the hand.

"Just don't make a mess of the couches," joked the driver as he reached for the door handle. "No dog hair on the upholstery, all right?"

Marcus coughed. "Ha. Well. I can't promise anything."

The driver pulled the door shut, leaving Marcus and Bobby alone in the dark.

# CHAPTER THIRTY-ONE

LAURA SAT ON HER COUCH IN FRONT OF THE TELE-vision. She was flicking back and forth between a base-ball game and a British crime drama. Her team was los-ing by a half-dozen runs in the fifth inning. The crime drama, well, she'd figured out who the murderer was in the first ten minutes of the show. She was about to switch off the TV when the phone rang.

"Hello?" she said, clicking the remote and tossing it aside.

"Hi, I'm looking for Laura," replied a woman's voice.

"This is Laura."

"Hi. You don't know me," said the woman. "My name is Beatrice. I have some information you need to know."

Laura laughed nervously. "What is this about?"

"Your son. John."

A long silence fell on the line.

"My son is dead," said Laura finally. Her voice was angry. "Don't call this number again."

She was about to hang up when Bea interrupted.

"Laura, he's alive," she blurted. "And so is Marcus. Laura, I know Marcus is a werewolf."

Laura choked on tears. "How could you know—"

"I'm sorry. I know this is hard," soothed Bea. "I believe you that Marcus is a werewolf because…." She paused a moment. "Because I'm a werewolf too."

"This is some kind of sick joke."

"It's no joke," said Bea. "John is alive and he's on his way to see you right now."

"He's on his way *here*?"

"Yes, right now. He wants to meet you. But, Laura…." Halfway across the country, Bea closed her eyes before continuing. "Marcus is following him. We think he's going to try to reach you before John can."

Laura sat on the couch. Her hand reached for her mouth. "No," she breathed. "He can't."

"I know this is a lot to take in, but I'm afraid Marcus is capable of almost anything, because he is very angry. And because…." Bea paused again. "Because tonight is the full moon."

Laura stood up and walked to the window. The sun hung low in the late-afternoon sky.

"Laura, I'm worried about you. And I'm worried about John. He's a werewolf, too. He's travelling with my niece, who is a…it's really complicated. I'm worried about all of you. Do you have someplace you can go?" asked Bea. "You have a bit of time. I don't think Marcus will be able to make it there until early morning."

Laura crossed the room to the bookshelf. She reached up to grab something from the top shelf.

"Laura, are you still there?"

"Oh, I'm here," said Laura calmly. She smoothed her hand over the lid of the cigar box. "No, I don't think I'll be going anywhere," she said. "I'll wait for Marcus right here."

"I don't think that's a good idea," cautioned Bea.

"I do," said Laura sharply. "What did you say your name was, again?"

"It's Beatrice. People call me Bea."

"Well, Bea," said Laura with a bitter laugh, "let me tell you a story."

# CHAPTER THIRTY-TWO

"STAND BACK," CAME MARCUS'S VOICE IN THE INKY darkness of the truck's trailer. "Stand against the door. I'm going to pull a couple of these couches down for us."

There was a noise of sliding, wood against wood, then a crash. Marcus swore quietly before dragging the furniture into position with a grunt.

"There."

Bobby felt his way through the dark to the seat of a brand new couch. The cushions were still wrapped in plastic. "Thanks," he said, settling in.

"Don't mention it. It's going to be a long ride."

"Why are you being nice to me?"

Marcus thought a moment. "Because I don't hate you, Bobby. I'm not a monster."

The engine of the truck roared to life. The sudden motion jostled Marcus and Bobby as the rig drove out of the parking lot and onto the highway.

"Then what am I doing here?" said Bobby.

"I couldn't exactly leave you at your house after you'd seen me," said Marcus. "As soon as Mummy and Daddy got home, you'd tell them exactly where I'd gone and what I was doing. It's just easier this way."

"What happens when we get where we're going?"

"To you? Nothing. I'm not going to hurt you."

"What about John and Kate?"

"What about them?"

Bobby could tell this question had angered him.

"What are you going to do to them?"

"That depends on them," said Marcus. "First, we need to get to that woman's house before they do. I don't know what happens after that."

The two sat in dark silence for a moment.

"What's wrong with John seeing his mom?" asked Bobby. "What's the big deal?"

"The big deal is that woman is a lunatic. She's dangerous," said Marcus.

"What do you mean?"

"She's the reason we've been on the run for fifteen years," said Marcus. Even in the dark, Bobby knew Marcus's face was twisted with rage.

"I don't understand."

"Don't you?" said Marcus. "Well, then. Let me tell you a story."

# CHAPTER THIRTY-THREE

"EVERYTHING WAS WONDERFUL," SAID LAURA ON the phone to Bea. "My friends thought I had it all. I had a great job. I had met and married this guy—this handsome and mysterious guy. And we had this beautiful baby boy. I can still see the light in Marcus's eyes when he first held John. You never saw a man so in love with his son."

"It was just like the movies," said Marcus in the darkness of the truck's trailer. "When I first met John's mum, it was just like that—instant connection. I loved her so much, and she seemed to love everything about me. Only she didn't know *everything* about me.

"Every month at the full moon, I found some reason to be gone. A business trip, a sick cousin, or whatever. And things just kept going. We got married. Bought a house. Had a baby. But she still didn't know the truth. She didn't know what I really was."

"At first, I didn't really think much about Marcus being gone so much," said Laura. "I mean, people travel for work, right? But after John was born, I had hoped all that would slow down, and we'd all spend more time together as a family. When I asked him about his trips or asked him to stay, he'd become moody and sullen. I had never seen him like that before."

"How many sick cousins can one guy have?" said Marcus miserably. "I knew I was going to have to tell her the truth. She had to know eventually anyway. There was a fifty-fifty chance John was going to be a werewolf. I just thought maybe it would be something she would accept and everything would be fine. I was so wrong."

"I was home alone with the baby one night," continued Laura. "Marcus was gone again. I remember there was this terrible storm. It rained so hard. The wind was howling. Around dusk, the storm knocked out the power. I brought the baby downstairs. I wrapped him in a blanket and laid him in the playpen. I lit some candles and settled into the rocking chair with a book. I didn't even hear Marcus come into the house. I just remember him standing in the doorway, dripping water all over the ground. He had this wild gleam in his eye I'd never seen before."

"I walk into the room and she gives me this look," said Marcus. "I could tell she was angry. She looked at me and just said, 'What are you doing home?' I told her there was something I had been keeping from her, and it didn't feel right. And she just stared at me.

"I didn't know how to say it. I was so nervous. All the words I'd practiced were gone. And then, before I had a chance to say anything, I heard it: the call. The sun must've gone down as I was waiting. I couldn't just ignore it. So I howled. Right there in the middle of the living room."

"And this man who I had always known to be gentle and loving and kind was making this terrible noise," said Laura. "It wasn't even human. And then," she continued, "he started to *change*. His eyes turned yellow, his teeth grew into the most terrifying fangs, and his body contorted until there was this snarling black wolf standing just a few feet from the baby—*my* baby."

"She was screaming," explained Marcus. "And she started throwing things at me. Anything she could get her hands on. Toys. Chairs. She threw a glass vase, which shattered and gashed me along my side. And then—I couldn't believe it—she grabbed a lit candle and threw it. I jumped out of the way and it landed on the ground right beside the playpen. A corner of a blanket was hanging over the edge—it caught fire like a torch."

"The baby was awake and crying," remembered Laura. "That monster was about to go for him, so I grabbed anything I could to throw. I threw a candle. The fire spread, and the wolf—Marcus—leapt into the playpen and grabbed John in his mouth."

"The playpen was on fire," said Marcus. "John was swaddled in his blanket. I picked him up. By the time I jumped out, the fire was spreading around the room. I ran out of the house with her chasing and throwing things at me."

"He took my baby," said Laura. "My *John*. He tore out of the room without even a look back and ran into the night. From all I knew, John was dead. That monster had killed him. The wolf disappeared into the woods, and I collapsed on the porch in tears."

"I hid with the baby until morning," said Marcus. "By then, she had already told the police. It was all over the news. '*Werewolf snatches baby*.' No one believed her, but there was no way I could go back.

"So I hit the road. I raised my son. I showed him the world. I made him who he is. And now, he's going to throw it all away." Marcus scoffed. "Imagine how she'll react when she discovers her precious son is a werewolf, too."

The trailer rocked gently back and forth. The muffled sound of the truck's engine roared briefly as the driver shifted gears.

"That's why I can't let them go back there."

"Fifteen years is a long time to live a nightmare, Bea."

Laura lifted the lid to the cigar box on her lap. She reached in and grasped the handle of the pistol inside.

"Which is why I intend to greet Marcus myself when he arrives. Maybe then I can make the nightmare stop."

# CHAPTER THIRTY-FOUR

"WE'RE CUTTING THIS AWFULLY CLOSE," WORRIED
Kate. She looked out the window of the train and watched
the Montreal skyline roll past. The sun was low in the sky,
painting the entire city in orange and pink. Kate would
have called it lovely if she weren't terrified of transform-
ing into a duck in the middle of a city of nearly two mil-
lion people. "How long until we arrive at the station?"

"About ten minutes," said John.

"And when does the sun go down?"

John looked at his watch. "In about fourteen
minutes."

"I knew it. I *knew* this was a bad plan," said Kate.

"Hey, relax," said John. "Nothing has changed."
He unzipped Kate's backpack and drew out a small
metal canteen. "Let's just drink the cure. If it doesn't
work, we've got Plan B." He patted Wacka's cage.
"Right, Wacka?"

"Wacka," said the duck.

John shook the canteen to mix its contents and unscrewed the lid.

"Here's to Plan A," he said, raising it to his lips. He drank deeply and made a sour face.

"Is it bad?" asked Kate.

John wiped his mouth with the back of his hand. "I've had worse."

He handed the canteen to Kate. She closed one eye and peeked inside. Chunks of herbs floated on top.

"Looks...gross," she said. She gave the canteen a quick sniff and scrunched her nose. "Smells worse." Kate pinched her nose and took a sip.

The cure was bitter and sweet at the same time. She choked down small pieces of root and herb. It tasted, in a word, brown.

"*When* have you tasted worse?" she asked.

"Okay, never," he said, taking back the canteen. "Wacka, your turn."

From another pocket in the backpack, he pulled out a medicine dropper. He fed bits of the cure to the duck, who didn't seem to find it nearly as distasteful as John and Kate had. She happily gobbled down several eyedroppers full.

"Feel any different?" asked Kate.

John shrugged.

"Me neither," said Kate. She looked up as someone approached.

"Well, my joyful travellers," said the moustached train conductor, sidling up to the space beside their seats. "I guess this is where we part ways."

"Oh, do you get off in Montreal?" asked Kate.

"This is my stop," said the conductor with a frown. "I get about eighteen hours of rest before climbing aboard another train to do the whole thing again." He looked at his watch. "Oh, by the way, we're running about ten minutes behind schedule."

Kate did some quick calculations in her head. "Wait," she said, casting a glance at John. "You mean everyone will still be on the train in fourteen minutes?"

The conductor chuckled. "Why, does something important happen in fourteen minutes?"

"Eleven, actually," said John with wide eyes.

"Well, yes then," said the conductor. "We won't pull into Montreal Station for another twenty minutes or so. Is that a problem?"

"Nope," blurted Kate stiffly, her eyes locked onto John's. "Everything is great. Thanks for asking."

"Okay, then," said the conductor, shifting uncomfortably from foot to foot. "I've a few jobs to take care of before we arrive. You're welcome to stay on the train during the stopover."

"Okay, great," managed Kate, still staring at John. "Thanks."

The conductor strode down the aisle, shaking his head.

"Okay, this is *really* not cool," said Kate. "I thought we'd at least be alone on an empty train when the sun went down."

"I know, I know," said John. He looked at his watch. "Nine minutes, by the way."

Kate's leg bumped up and down as the minutes ticked by. The passengers around them were gathering their bags, preparing to get off the train when they arrived at the station.

"How much longer?"

"About a minute," said John. He looked out the window. The fading rays of the sun were blocked by the city skyline. "Feeling anything?"

"Feeling *terrified,* thank you," said Kate. Her heart raced. "This is going to work, right?" she demanded. "Tell me the cure will work."

"I can't do that," answered John. "Just be cool. We have a backup plan."

John's red face betrayed his calming words. He glanced at his watch every few seconds. Kate could see he was just as nervous as she was.

"Okay," he said, looking one last time at his watch. "Sun's down."

"You're sure?" asked Kate.

He nodded.

Kate breathed a long sigh of relief. "Oh, thank god."

John cracked a smile. "Let's hear it for Plan A," he said.

They both laughed.

"It worked!" whooped Kate.

"I knew it would," said John with a casual shrug.

"This is so cool!" began Kate. "When we get back, we'll have to tell Netty that—"

She stopped short, interrupted by a familiar voice.

*"Whooooo?"*

The call of the moon.

"No!" shouted Kate. Several passengers turned to look at her.

"It didn't work," whispered John, suddenly frantic.

*"Whooooo?"*

Kate felt her face break out into beads of sweat. She *needed* to answer the call. She gripped the armrests of her seat. John cast about listlessly.

"Plan B," Kate said firmly.

John's eyes darted around the car. He shifted in his seat. He hadn't heard her.

"Plan B," Kate repeated, a little louder.

"I don't know if I can," he hissed. "I need to answer *now*."

"No," said Kate. "John, don't. Calm down and look at me."

"*Whooooo?*" called the moon.

John's body jerked in response.

"John, *look* at me," said Kate again.

John's eyes locked onto Kate's. His expression pleaded for help.

"You can do this," said Kate. "*We* can do this. Grab the bag. I'll grab Wacka. Let's go."

John stood up and reached with a shaking hand for the backpack. He slung it over his shoulder. Kate stood up and picked up Wacka's cage.

"Now, walk to the back of the car," said Kate into John's ear.

John walked up the aisle, pausing every few steps when the call of the moon overcame him. The train rolled slowly past parked freight cars in a railway yard.

"Ladies and gentlemen, we are now approaching Montreal Station," said a voice over the train's loud-speaker. "Please stay seated until we've come to a complete stop, at which point you may gather your belongings and make your way to the platform. Thank you for travelling Via Rail. Have a great evening."

The passengers ignored the instructions to remain in their seats and stood up. John was so overcome by the call of the moon, he had frozen in place three seats from the rear of the car. A man and woman in the seat immediately beside him tried to push into the aisle.

"Excuse us," said Kate. She put her free hand on John's back and gave him a shove, launching him past the couple.

"Well, I never!" said the woman.

"You sure haven't," responded Kate, opening the door to the tiny bathroom at the back of the car. She pushed John inside, stepped in after him, and shut the door.

"Good gracious!" cried the woman, looking at the bathroom door. "What in the world do you suppose—"

Her words were cut short as the train plunged into the darkness of the underground station. The passengers collectively gasped. A few laughed nervously when, seconds later, the lights came on.

"Did you hear that?" said the woman to her husband.

"Hear what?" he said.

"It just—" she began. "It almost sounded, just a second ago, like a wolf howling."

Her husband took the luggage from her hand and slung it over his shoulder. He gently patted her on the back.

"You've been on the train too long, my dear."

# CHAPTER THIRTY-FIVE

MARCUS'S HOWL ECHOED OFF THE WALLS OF THE truck's trailer. The timbre and tone of his voice became animal as his body transformed into that of a wolf. He paced restlessly for a few minutes—his claws clicking on the steel floor of the trailer—before returning to his spot on his couch.

Bobby took a deep breath. Marcus might be a giant wolf, but somehow that put Bobby at ease. He'd grown up with wolves his whole life. Sure, they could be dangerous, but there was one thing they couldn't do: talk back.

"There's some stuff I don't get," said Bobby. "I've been thinking about your story. I don't really get why adults do a lot of things, but I think maybe this is different. You're mad at my family because you think we stole John," he said. "But you, like, *abandoned* him in the middle of nowhere. I don't get that."

Bobby thought for a minute before continuing. "And that reporter guy? He was going to put us on the front page of his newspaper because of you. But when your plan didn't work, you got mad at *us*. I don't get that either."

He sat forward on the couch, feeling surer of his words.

"And John's mom? That must have been really scary for you. But, like, what about her? She didn't even know there was such a thing as werewolves, and all of a sudden, one shows up and takes her baby away. And you're mad at *her*?"

Bobby paused briefly to think.

"Maybe I'm just a kid, and maybe I should just shut up. But I think you look around and see nothing but bad guys," he said. "Marcus, if this was a story, *you'd* be the bad guy."

The truck swayed gently back and forth as it hurtled down the highway.

"I used to think there were real good guys and real bad guys, just like in books," said Bobby. "I don't think that anymore. I think everyone believes they're the good guy in their own story, and everyone who wants something different is a bad guy."

Bobby wondered if he'd already said too much. Marcus hadn't stirred since he began talking.

"My family has done stuff you don't like, but that doesn't make us bad guys. You've done some awful stuff, but y'know what? I don't think you're the bad guy either," said Bobby. He settled back into his seat on the couch. "At least, you don't have to be."

# CHAPTER THIRTY-SIX

"EXCUSE ME. SORRY. EXCUSE ME."

Dirk Bragg squeezed through the narrow aisle of the train. He glanced right and left as he walked, giving each passenger a quick once-over. He'd travelled nearly the length of the train in search of those kids. He was beginning to wonder if this was a wasted trip.

He paused briefly beside a set of four empty seats. A sweater sat balled up the corner. A half-empty bag of chips lay on the table. *Barbecue*, thought Dirk. *Could be them*. He made a mental note to return here once he'd finished his sweep of the train.

The next car, the last on the train, was empty. The back was cluttered with a pile of oversized duffle bags and dozens of hockey sticks. Dirk decided these belonged to the rowdy men in ball caps he'd seen in one of the forward cars—a hockey team travelling to a tournament.

"Sir," came a voice from behind Dirk. "Sir, this car is closed."

Dirk turned to find a female conductor standing at the entrance to the car.

"I'm sorry," he replied. "I didn't realize."

"No problem, sir," she said. "Could I see your ticket?"

Dirk searched his pockets for the stub of paper and handed it over.

"Heading to Moncton?" she said, reading the ticket.

"Yes, ma'am," he replied. "You haven't seen a pair of teenagers on board, have you? My niece and nephew were supposed to be on this train."

"I haven't run across any teenagers travelling alone," she replied, "but I just came aboard in Montreal. Tell you what: when I find them, I'll tell them you're looking for them. What did you say their names were?"

"Kate and John," said Dirk with a grin. "And please, don't tell them I'm looking for them. I'd like it to be a surprise."

"Kate and John," she repeated, handing back his ticket. "Now, I'm going to have to ask you to find a seat in another car. We're closing this one off."

Dirk followed her through the double doors to the next car. Whoever was sitting in the seats of four hadn't returned, so he took an empty seat across the aisle.

Dirk opened the flap on his old knapsack and peered inside. Despite his repeated vow to become a more organized packer, he had stuffed his bag at the last minute with objects that made sense at the time, but now just seemed odd. Why would he need a field guide to the fungi of Southeast Asia? And of course he would need deodorant on this trip, but on reflection, six sticks of Old Spice seemed excessive. He pushed items aside, including a ceremonial key to the city of Cincinnati—an artefact he'd come across while investigating reports of zombie activity in Ohio—and finally found what he was looking for: the one banana that had evaded Canadian customs. A lovely specimen, not too ripe, with a touch of green at the tip. For all its jostling in his bag, it was perfect: not a bruise on it. He was just about to break into the peel when he heard a commotion from the back of the car.

"Oh, my goodness!" gasped a woman. "Is that a wolf?"

Dirk swivelled in his seat, along with every other passenger in the car. A teenage girl in dark sunglasses stood in the doorway to the bathroom. In one hand, she held a small pet carrier. In the other, she grasped a harness attached to a large service dog. It did, indeed, look a lot like a wolf.

"I'M BLIND!" exclaimed the girl in a voice that was just a bit too loud. "THIS IS MY DOG!"

A grin spread across Dirk's face as the girl's "service dog" guided her up the aisle. Dirk couldn't see the creature inside the pet carrier, but he was sure it was more likely to quack than meow.

"I'M BLIND!" repeated the girl as she walked up the aisle.

The commotion among the passengers faded to sympathy. An older man stood up. "Can I help you find your seat, young lady?" he said.

"I'M FINE!" she said. "I'M BLIND!"

The "dog"—John—led her to the seats immediately across from Dirk. She set the pet carrier on the seat nearest the window and sat beside it. John curled up on the floor beneath her feet.

Dirk chuckled as he realized the girl had left two empty seats across from her. He scooted across the aisle.

"Mind if I join you?" he said, not waiting for her answer before sitting down.

John recognized Dirk right away. He growled.

"My, my," said Dirk to Wacka. "Your dog seems a bit jumpy."

Wacka thought frantically. This man was familiar. Was he the same man who tried to get Kate in trouble last summer? John didn't seem to like him....

"HE'S FINE," she said. "I'M BLIND."

"Yes, you mentioned that. And may I say hello to your cat?" Dirk peered into the carrier and found exactly what he was expecting. "Oh, goodness me. *That's* not a cat at all."

"THIS IS MY DUCK!" shouted the girl.

"I can see that," said Dirk. He leaned forward to whisper into the cage. "Hi there, Kate. It's nice to see you again."

Kate looked up into the smirking face of Dirk Bragg—the reporter she and John had come to know as Dirt Bag.

Plan B was going off the rails.

# CHAPTER THIRTY-SEVEN

"SO," SAID DIRK, HIS VOICE DRIPPING WITH HONEY, "if we're going to be seatmates for this trip, let's get to know each other, shall we? My name's Dirk. What's yours?"

"WACKA," exclaimed Wacka.

John pawed at her leg. "WENDY!" she corrected. "MY NAME IS WENDY. I'M BLIND."

"Well, then," said Dirk. "Nice to meet you, Wacka-Wendy. Now, what are you doing on this train with my friends Kate and John?"

Wacka shifted uncomfortably in her seat. Kate and John had assured her she wouldn't have to speak very much. They'd promised that people would leave her alone. This man was asking a lot of questions.

"I AM ON A TRIP," she said, repeating the lines Kate had drilled into her. "THIS IS MY DOG. THIS IS MY DUCK."

"Right," said Dirk. "But where are you going?"

Wacka scowled and tilted her head. "I AM ON A TRIP."

"Yes, but where are you *going* on your trip?" insisted Dirk. "What is your destination?"

Wacka wracked her brain for useful information. This man was asking too many questions. She did not want to talk to him anymore.

"I'M TIRED NOW!" announced Wacka, remembering another of her prepared lines. "I'M TIRED, AND I'M BLIND!" She leaned against the pet carrier and began to make what she believed were convincing human sleeping noises.

*"SNOOOXXX,"* she snored. *"SNOOOXXXX!"*

Dirk sighed and leaned forward to address Kate. "Your friend is a bit peculiar, Kate," he said, "but that's fine. I'm sure we'll get to know each other. Saaaaaay," he continued with a grin, "you didn't happen to catch that article I wrote about you, did you? I thought it turned out kind of nice."

Kate quacked. Had Dirk understood the language of ducks, he would have known he'd just been sworn at.

"The sun comes up before we hit Moncton," whispered Dirk, digging something out of his bag. "I'm sure we can have a nice chat then about what you're all doing."

Dirk withdrew his camera from his bag and pointed it through the bars of Kate's cage.

"Smile!"

Dirk clicked the shutter on his camera several times and set it aside. He grinned widely, leaned back in his seat, and closed his eyes.

# CHAPTER THIRTY-EIGHT

"YOUR ATTENTION, PLEASE," CAME A VOICE OVER the train's loudspeaker. "Sorry for the interruption, folks. We'll be pulling into Moncton in about twenty minutes. Moncton Station, twenty minutes."

Kate peered out of her cage at Dirk. A cold shudder ran through her. Who would have thought such a dufus could throw her life into such chaos? His head was turned at an awkward angle, his cheek pressed into the headrest. His eyes were closed and his mouth hung wide open.

It had been a long, sleepless night. The train was still dark. If they were getting close to Moncton, it meant they had travelled all night through Quebec and northern New Brunswick. Sunrise was only about a half-hour away.

John, however, was wide awake. He uncurled himself from his spot on the floor and reached across the aisle to grab a magazine from under the seat opposite. It was an issue of *Cosmo*. Kate thought it was an odd time for a werewolf to start thinking about fashion trends and relationship quizzes.

John laid the magazine in front of Kate's cage. He used his paw to cover up every letter of the title but the first. "C."

He winked, hoping his message was clear.

*Plan C,* thought Kate.

She stared into the wolf's eyes. He was confident. Almost smiling. Without words, there was no way he could communicate what his new plan was. If they were going to do this, she was just going to have to trust him. Again.

She nodded.

John turned to Wacka, who sat sleeping in her chair. He pressed his cold nose into the back of her hand.

"I'M BLIND," she groaned.

Kate hissed a quiet warning. Wacka's eyes flew open and darted from the duck in the cage to the sleeping reporter. Dirt Bag shifted in his seat, rolling his head to face the other direction. "I swear," he mumbled, "I swear it was a duck." His eyes remained closed. Wacka, John, and Kate waited until they heard his steady breathing resume.

John gently tugged Wacka's shirtsleeve. She stood up, slung John's backpack over her shoulder, and carefully picked up Kate's cage.

John led them through the rows of sleeping passengers. Wacka opened the back door and walked through to the space between cars. The *click-click, click-clack* of the wheels rolling on the rails rattled through the space. A red-and-white sign on the outside door read: *WARNING! Do not open while train is in motion.*

"Quack," quacked Kate. She had a sudden feeling John's Plan C involved not heeding that warning. She had no desire to jump out of a moving train.

John ignored her and pawed instead at the door that led to the next car. Wacka opened it. It was empty. John led them to the back, past the door of the tiny bathroom. He began to dig at the mountain of hockey gear, trying to expose the back door of the train.

"KATIE," said Wacka. "KATIE, WHAT IS JOHN DOING?"

Kate quacked. Wacka lifted the latch on her cage, and Kate waddled out. John pawed hockey sticks away from the door and dragged a hockey bag from the top of the pile with his teeth.

"Well, well, well," came a voice from behind them. "Thought you might get away before the sun came up, did you?" Dirt Bag stood smirking at the front of the car. His camera strap was wrapped around his wrist. He looked at his watch. "Oh, and look at that. It's almost sunrise."

Dirk raised the camera and pointed it at them. "We'll call these the 'before' shots for the front cover of *Really Real News*," he said, clicking the shutter over and over, "and, just maybe, *The New York Times*." He lowered the camera. His smirk had faded to a scowl. "No one believed me when I tried to tell the truth about you. They all thought it was all some big joke. Nobody will be laughing this time, when I expose you for what you *really* are, you filthy, no-good—"

"KATIE, I DON'T LIKE THIS MAN!" yelled Wacka.

Dirk strode down the aisle toward them. "Ah, yes. Our blind friend," said Dirk. "I can't quite figure out what role you play in all of this."

"I'M BLIND!" exclaimed Wacka.

"Riiiiight," said Dirk, rolling his eyes. He made a quick jump toward her. She flinched. "Nope," he said, plucking the sunglasses off her face. "How'd you get mixed up with a couple of mangy werekids?"

John growled.

"Ooooh, the big bad wolf," teased Dirk. He snapped a photo of John's snarling face. "Oh, yeah, that's a good one. Lots of teeth. People will be—"

Kate had had enough. She flew at Dirk, quacking and scratching at him with her feet.

"Hey! What the—"

Dirk waved his arms wildly at the flailing duck. Kate's wings knocked the camera from his hands. As Wacka leaned over to pick it up, John leap-frogged over her and grabbed Dirk by the pant leg.

"Hey!" he cried again. "Let go!"

John pulled him by the hem of his pants to the back of the car, with Kate offering aerial support.

Wacka stood up, examining the camera like it was some kind of foreign object. She pointed it at Dirk's face and clicked the shutter.

"DIE, ALIEN SCUM!" she cried. The flash blinded Dirk as the shutter clicked again and again.

Dirk tripped backward over John. He landed with his back against the bathroom door. John lunged again, pushing Dirk through the door and onto the floor of the bathroom.

"Get off of me!" yelled Dirk as he struggled against the wolf.

Kate could see what John had in mind. She hopped up onto the pile of hockey gear and quacked furiously to get Wacka's attention.

Dirk yowled in pain as John's teeth sunk into his ankle. He wrenched Dirk the rest of the way into the bathroom. The door slammed behind him.

"ALIEN SCUM!" yelled Wacka, sliding a hockey stick into the door handle, locking it shut.

The door jiggled furiously as Dirk tried to open it. The hockey stick was holding for now, but might slip out of place at any moment.

"Hey! What's going on?" yelled Dirk. "Let me out of here!"

"Quack!" exclaimed Kate. She looked out the windows and saw a faint glow in the sky. Sunrise was only moments away. It was time to do something drastic. They needed to get off the train.

Kate quacked again and took off flying over the rows of empty seats toward the front of the car.

"KATIE, WAIT!" yelled Wacka, running after. John bounded along behind them. They passed through the door leading to the space between cars. The *clickety-clack* roared in their ears.

"Quack!" said Kate, hopping onto the handle of the outside door. "Quack, quack, quack!"

John leaped up to push the door open with his front paws. The door slid aside, revealing a rush of trees and gravel moving past. The open door triggered an alarm that buzzed throughout the train.

Wacka stared out the door with wide eyes. "KATIE WANT WACKA TO *JUMP?*"

Kate gulped. Even with the train moving slowly jumping seemed reckless, but they needed to get away. Now.

Wacka grasped a metal railing with one hand and leaned outside. She peered in the direction they were travelling.

"KATIE! KATIE!" she exclaimed over the sound of the train. "LOOK, KATIE! RIVER!"

Kate poked out her head and saw a green sign whiz past with the words *Boundary Creek* painted in white. The train was approaching a bridge spanning a small river.

"KATIE!" exclaimed Wacka, picking up Kate. "WACKA JUMP! WACKA HOLD KATIE!"

Wacka grasped Kate in one arm and held onto the metal railing with the other. John stood beside her, ready to jump. Air rushing past rippled his fur. They were nearly there. The wind roared in their ears. There was no time to reconsider.

"ONE," began Wacka, rocking back and forth. "TWO...." The bank of the river whooshed past. It was time. "THREE!"

Wacka, John, and Kate leaped from the train. They fell through the cool morning air, plunging toward the surface of the water dozens of metres below.

Dirk gripped the latch of the bathroom door and gave it one final tug. He collapsed backward onto the sink as the hockey stick rattled free and the door swung in. Dirk climbed over the stick and ran up the aisle after the kids, limping slightly from the bite on his ankle.

He entered the space between cars and found the outside door hanging wide open. That would explain the incessant alarm.

*Could they have jumped?* wondered Dirk. *Even at this speed, it would be suicide.* He leaned out the door to see if he could spot anything.

"Sir!" shouted a stern voice from behind him. "Sir, step away from the door!"

Dirk turned to find a uniformed security officer staring at him.

"It's not what you think—" began Dirk.

"I think a whole lot of things," said the officer, eyeing Dirk suspiciously. "Step away from the door."

Dirk obeyed. The officer leaned past him to pull the door closed. The buzzing alarm stopped. He reached for his walkie-talkie.

"Yeah, this is Boudreau," said the officer, one eye still on Dirk as if he thought he might make a run for it. "I've secured the door. Everything is locked down."

"Really, it's not what you think. I didn't open the door."

"Sure you didn't," replied Boudreau.

"I didn't!" insisted Dirk. "It was…that blind girl… and her wolf…and the duck. They must have jumped."

Boudreau stared blankly at Dirk. "A blind girl with a duck and a wolf jumped from the train?" he repeated.

"Yes," said Dirk confidently.

"Okay," said Boudreau. He reached again for his walkie-talkie. "I'm going to need a bit of backup here. We've got a live one."

# CHAPTER THIRTY-NINE

ERNIE HIT THE "SCAN" BUTTON ON THE RADIO OF his truck. Driving a big rig back and forth across the country like he did, it seemed like every time he found a good classic rock station, he lost the signal a few minutes later. He let the radio cycle through the dial a few times before settling on a station playing an AC/DC tune.

Ernie nodded his head to the beat and hummed a few bars of the guitar riff. He'd been driving all night and needed loud, energetic music to keep him awake. A faint glow in the east showed sunrise wasn't far off. Just a few more hours on the road, and he'd be in Halifax. He'd unload his trailer, grab some grub, and find a parking lot where he could sleep for a few hours.

He spotted a sign announcing the big truck stop just before Moncton. He looked at his gas gauge and decided he had enough to make it the rest of the way to Halifax. No need to stop just yet.

He was about to breeze past the exit when he remembered his passengers in the back.

"Aw, shoot," he said, engaging the engine brakes. The engine roared in protest as the truck slowed enough for him to steer onto the exit ramp.

"Boundary Creek," he muttered to himself, glancing at the map sitting on the seat beside him. It was just a stone's throw from the highway. He'd be there in a few minutes.

Ernie drove along the country road in the early morning darkness. He wasn't sure exactly where in Boundary Creek these folks wanted to be dropped off. He slowed the truck to halt beside the sign that marked the edge of the community. He killed the engine. The sudden quiet engulfed the peaceful stretch of road.

Ernie climbed down from the cab and walked around to the back of the truck. He had hesitated when the guy asked him for a ride, but this errand turned out to be no big deal. The two hundred bucks the guy offered sure didn't hurt. Maybe this time he'd order the *big* breakfast.

He unlocked the latch on the door and pulled it open.

"Okey-dokey," he announced. "Boundary Creek. Not sure where you guys—"

Ernie froze in terror as he found himself staring into the yellow eyes of a giant, fearsome, black wolf. The wolf lowered its face to Ernie's and let out a low growl.

Ernie stumbled backward onto the gravel shoulder of the road. "No!" he shouted, scrambling away on his hands and knees. "No! Get away! Get *away*!"

The wolf jumped down from the trailer; the boy climbed down after.

"It's okay," said Bobby. "He's not going to hurt you. Just...go back to your truck. You never saw us, okay?"

Ernie wrenched around to look at the wolf. Marcus growled again.

"I never saw nothin'!" Ernie shouted, his eyes full of fear. He scrambled to his feet and ran towards the cab of his truck. "Just leave me alone!" The engine roared to life before Ernie had even pulled the door closed.

Marcus stopped growling, turned to Bobby, and nodded. The small pack strapped around Marcus's chest holding his clothes was a bit snug. He twisted his body to give himself more breathing space.

Marcus glanced around to get his bearings. It had been years since he had been in this place, but he knew exactly where he was. When he and John had spent last summer in New Brunswick, he'd scanned the phone book to confirm Laura still lived at the same address. He'd be at her house in minutes. He only hoped he would arrive before John.

# CHAPTER FORTY

LAURA HADN'T SLEPT AT ALL. SHE SAT MOTION-less in her chair, watching the back door. Her hand gripped the revolver, waiting for the sun to rise, which, to her relief, looked as if it was about to happen. It was some comfort knowing that when her nightmare arrived, it would at least be in human form. Maybe she wouldn't need the gun after all.

She stood up and walked to the screen door. She scanned the line of trees that marked the edge of her backyard where the forest began.

She gasped.

Just a moment before, there had been nothing but shadows. Now there stood the hulking silhouette of a wolf. It stared at her from the darkness. The wolf stepped out of the brush at the edge of the forest and into the dim light of dawn.

It was *him*. Fear rushed through every part of her body. She shook and trembled as if had been mere seconds and not fifteen years since that awful night. She clenched her teeth and turned her fear into anger.

Laura raised her hand and pointed the heavy revolver at the wolf. The creature cocked its head to one side.

Laura closed her eyes and pulled the trigger.

The explosion from the gun was louder than she expected. The metal became hot in her hands. She opened her eyes and saw her bullet had hit its mark. The wolf's crumpled body lay motionless in the grass.

She pushed open the screen door as the sun peeked over the horizon. As she strode across the yard, the wolf seemed to melt into the form of a man lying on his side, blood staining his shoulder and arm. As Laura came closer, she saw he didn't have the black hair she was expecting, but rusty brown. The realization hit her like a bag of bricks.

It wasn't Marcus.

"Wacka, I think he's over here!" shouted a girl's voice from the woods. "John! What was that sound?"

A young teenaged girl with dark hair emerged from the forest. She was just fastening the top button of her shirt when she saw Laura standing over the body of her best friend.

"John!" she gasped.

Kate dashed to John's side and rolled him over.

"John, no! Say something!"

John coughed. "Kate?" he said weakly.

"I'm here. Yes, it's Kate." She placed her hand on his wounded shoulder.

Laura stood frozen in the middle of the yard. The gun dangled from her fingertips, then dropped to the grass.

"John?" Laura whispered. She fell to her knees. "I shot...John? But...how can that—"

"We have to move him into the house," said Kate.

Laura seemed to come out of a trance. "Yes," she said. "Yes, of course." She hurried to Kate's side. "How can we move him?"

Kate looked John up and down. "I think...you grab his legs, I'll hold onto his chest, and we'll haul him in."

They got into position, but John cried in pain as they tried to lift him. Kate looked helpless. "What are we going to do?"

"Don't move him," said a man's voice.

Laura looked up to see Marcus rushing toward them from the side of the house. "Stay away!" she shouted. "Stay away or I'll...."

"Or what?" he challenged. "Or he dies?"

Marcus kneeled beside John.

"Dad?" said John in a small voice. He coughed again. "I'm cold."

"I'm here," said Marcus. "Everything's going to be okay. I've got you."

"Dad...."

Marcus turned to Kate. "Can you find me some blankets? Quickly?"

Kate nodded and ran into the house.

"Let's see what you've got here," said Marcus. John winced as his father gently turned him over. "The bullet went clean through," he said to himself.

"I thought he was you, Marcus," said Laura. "I thought you were coming back to kill me. I never meant...."

Marcus nodded.

"Silver bullet?" he asked.

"Yes," she replied.

"Good. Then he has a chance."

Laura stared at him. "Good?" she stammered. "But...."

Kate ran back from the house with a blue wool blanket. She helped Laura wrap it around John's shivering body.

"The cure," said Marcus to Kate. "Do you still have some?"

Kate looked at him blankly. "What?"

"The Cure for Werewolf, do you have any left?"

"I...I think so," she said. "It's in my canteen."

Kate ran to the woods and searched the ground. Wacka had been carrying the canteen when they emerged from the river, but must have dropped it in the forest when she turned back into a duck.

*Where is Wacka?* thought Kate. She worried about her friend for just a moment before she spotted a corner of the canteen poking out of a bed of ferns. She grabbed it and rushed it back to Marcus.

"There's not much left," she said. "Just a few swallows."

"It'll be enough," he said, taking the canteen from her. Marcus unscrewed the lid. "John," he said with a grimace, "I'm sorry. This is going to hurt."

John moaned and whispered, "Daddy, no...."

Marcus held the mouth of the canteen over the bullet hole and began to pour. What looked like steam sizzled from the wound. John screamed in pain as Marcus began to recite:

*"If the wolf you seek to calm,*
*Let this potion be your guide:*
*A shot of silver, a soothing balm;*
*Still the beast that lives inside."*

"Marcus, what are you doing?" shouted Kate.

"Saving his life," said Marcus, emptying the canteen on John's shoulder.

John lay writhing on the ground. "Stop!" he shouted, his voice cracking. "Dad, stop!"

Marcus dropped the empty canteen and put his hands on his son.

"I'm done now," he soothed. "Daddy's all done. Lie back."

John's face was streaked with tears. "Dad!" he gasped in pain and terror, still rocking back and forth.

But Kate could see something was happening. John's breathing was calming down. His violent shaking was slowing. Kate held her breath.

John curled up into a ball on the ground, wrapping his arms around his body. When his hand brushed his injured shoulder, he stopped.

"Dad," he said steadily. He sat up. "Dad, what the heck?"

"What is it?" said Kate, leaning in to get a better look.

John pulled his hand away. The wound was gone. In its place was a pink welt, like an old, faded scar.

"It's gone!" said Kate. She laughed nervously. "Are you okay?"

"I'm...fine. But...." He looked at Marcus. "Dad, what happened?"

"The cure," said Marcus simply, picking up the empty canteen and screwing the lid back on. "It saved your life." He paused a second. "Mostly."

"Mostly?" asked John.

"It saved the human part of you," explained Marcus. "We were really lucky to have this. But I'm afraid the wolf in you is gone. Forever."

# CHAPTER FORTY-ONE

BOBBY RAN AS FAST AS HIS SNEAKERS COULD CARRY him. His feet pounded the sidewalk as he tore around the quiet suburb, looking for his sister and John. He'd lost Marcus ages ago. When Bobby last saw him, he was running toward this neighbourhood. But Marcus was much faster on four legs than Bobby was on two.

Then, a little while later, he'd heard a loud *BANG.* He prayed it wasn't a gunshot, but he knew in his heart that it was.

Bobby rounded a corner. Every house in this neighbourhood looked the same. Every window was still dark. Dozens of questions raced through Bobby's mind. How would he be able to find out which house they were in? What *was* that shot? Was John okay? Was *Katie* okay?

Bobby stopped at an intersection. He looked right and left. To his left, the road ended in a cul-de-sac near a small forest. At the last house on the block, he spotted a man and a woman sitting on the porch. Bobby ran toward them. That shot must have been nearly half an hour ago but he was having trouble keeping track of time. Maybe they'd seen or heard something.

The couple on the front porch watched him approach. The man stood up. Bobby did a double take when he realized it was Marcus.

"I was wondering when you'd show up," he called, stepping off the porch to greet him. His face wore an expression Bobby had never seen on it before. He was smiling.

"I heard a shot," said Bobby, pausing to catch his breath. "Is everyone okay?"

"Everyone's fine," said Marcus. He looked from Bobby to Laura sitting on the porch. "Everyone is going to be fine."

Bobby looked confused.

"Sorry. Bobby, this is Laura. Laura, this is the young man I was telling you about."

"Nice to meet you, Bobby," said Laura, standing to shake his hand.

Bobby's eyes bulged. He turned to Marcus. "Like, *Laura* Laura?"

Marcus nodded.

"The lady you were telling me about?"

"The very same."

Bobby blinked. "John's mum?"

"That's her."

"And you're just sitting with her, chatting pleasantly on the porch like everything is totally *fine*?"

Laura grinned. Marcus coughed.

"Well," said Marcus with a wry smile. "A lot has happened in the last half hour."

Bobby looked back and forth from Marcus to Laura. "I'm so confused right now," he said. "I thought you guys, like, *hated* each other."

"Hate is such a strong word," said Marcus.

"More like, deplored," corrected Laura.

Marcus and Laura exchanged a glance and laughed.

"Can somebody tell me what's going on?" demanded Bobby.

"Honestly, I'm not quite sure myself," said Marcus, "but you're right. We did hate each other. But now...."

"Now we're just," said Laura with a shrug, "catching up. Sorting out the last fifteen years."

"This is so weird," said Bobby, shaking his head.

"It *is* weird," agreed Marcus. "But it's good, too. And really, the one person we have to thank for this... is you, Bobby."

Bobby took a step back. "Me?"

"You," said Marcus. He smiled.

Bobby thought for a moment. "I still don't get it."

"You helped me look at our story in a different way, Bobby," said Marcus. "I never stopped to think of how my actions affected the people around me. Your family. John." He paused. "Laura." He turned and held her gaze a moment.

"And so everything is...better now?" ventured Bobby.

"I still think there's a lot of talking and healing that has to happen," said Laura, "but yes. Things are definitely better now."

"Are you guys, like, back together then?"

Laura and Marcus laughed awkwardly. "I don't know if we've come *that* far," said Marcus. "But we've come to an understanding. John's going to live here with his mum."

"Really?" said Bobby, turning to Laura. "You don't mind living with a werewolf?"

"I can't wait to have him live with me," she said, beaming. "But John isn't a werewolf. Not anymore."

Bobby stared. "*What*?"

"It's a long story, Bobby," said Marcus, "and one Kate and John can fill you in on. But yes. John won't ever be a werewolf again."

"Is he okay?" asked Bobby anxiously.

"He's fine," Laura reassured him. "You can go in and see him, if you like. He's resting in his room upstairs."

Bobby put his hand on the door handle. Marcus spoke before he could enter.

"I don't know how to properly thank you, Bobby," he said. "I've been wrong about a lot of things for a very long time, and you helped me see that. So, thank you."

"You're welcome," said Bobby. "I guess."

"And I'm sorry," said Marcus. "I'm sorry for everything I've done to you and your family. I hope you can forgive me."

Bobby looked up at him. "Where are you going to go now?"

"Oh, I'll be around," he said. "It's probably best I hit the road again. But I'm sure we'll see each other again." Marcus thought a moment. "You were right about me," he said. "I don't have to be the bad guy. But I know one thing for sure: you're the good guy, Bobby."

"I swear, one day you will be the death of me, Katie Wereduck," said Kate's mother over the phone later that morning.

Kate winced. She hadn't heard her mother this upset in years. Maybe ever. "I know," she said into the receiver. "I'm so sorry."

"Your father and I were worried *sick*," scolded Lisa. "And on a full-moon night, of all nights. Your father paced around the house all night, growling at anything that moved."

"Oh, Mum," said Kate. "I don't know what to say...."

"But," interrupted her mother, her tone changing. "I'm glad you're safe. And I'm glad you were able to help John reconnect with his mother. That took a lot of courage. You've been a good friend to him."

Kate blushed. "Thanks, Mum."

In the background, Kate could hear her father shouting.

"Did you tell her about the *pacing* and the *growling* and how we were worried SICK ABOUT HER?" he yelled.

Lisa put her hand over the receiver but Kate could still hear her mother's retort: "Brian, she's *fine*. Calm down and go get a cup of tea."

Kate smiled.

"Can I speak to your brother?" said Lisa.

"Sure thing. I think he just ate half the food in Laura's fridge."

Kate passed the phone to Bobby.

"Mum! I rode in the back of an eighteen-wheeler and it was AWESOME!"

Kate knocked on the bedroom door and pushed it open a crack.

"Mind if I come in?" she asked.

John propped himself up on his pillow. "No, it's fine," he said. "Come on in."

Kate entered and sat on the edge of his bed. "You okay?"

"Much better," he said, rubbing his shoulder. "How was it on the phone with your parents?"

"They...weren't the happiest with me. But they understand why we did it."

John raised his eyebrows. "That's cool."

"Yeah."

They sat quietly for a moment. Kate looked around the room. Morning sunlight poured through a window over a small, wooden desk. On the desktop was a framed photo of a laughing baby John and a much younger-looking Laura. Her eyes were so happy—like nothing bad could ever happen to her and her perfect son. And now they were reunited. John was here to stay.

"So, this is great," said Kate to John. "Right? I mean, this is what you wanted?"

"I guess so," he replied. "I mean, I'm not a werewolf anymore, so maybe it makes sense that I live with my not-werewolf mom."

Kate's eyes welled up.

"I understand," she said. "And what if...what if there were some werewolves—and maybe a duck or two—who missed you?"

John grabbed Kate's hand. "I think a not-werewolf guy could still be best friends with a duck," he said softly.

"You'll be so far away," sniffed Kate.

"But see," he said, leaning back on his pillows with a grin, "they invented this thing called the internet."

Kate laughed. "I guess. But we have to chat every day. Promise?"

"Promise."

Bobby barged into the room and tossed the cordless phone on the bed. "Hey."

"Don't worry, you weren't interrupting or anything," said Kate sarcastically.

Bobby scoffed. "When have I ever worried about that?"

Kate and John laughed.

"Can I ask a dumb question?" said Bobby. "Where's Wacka?"

"Oh, my gosh!" exclaimed Kate. "Wacka!"

Kate dashed out of the room and down the stairs. She flew out the back door and ran into the yard.

"Waaaaacka!" She pushed through branches at the edge of the forest. "Wacka, where are you?"

Kate traced her steps to the spot where she'd found her canteen. She couldn't see Wacka anywhere. She called for the duck as she pushed deeper into the forest toward the river.

"Wacka," quacked a familiar voice, just to Kate's right.

Kate followed her friend's quacks until she found her nested in the dry leaves at the base of a tree; she was wrapped loosely in some sort of leather strap. Kate's backpack lay nearby.

"There you are," said Kate, kneeling beside the duck. "What have you got?"

Kate freed the duck from the strap. A grin spread across her face when she realized what it was attached to.

"Oh, sweetie," she said with a laugh. "You got Dirt Bag's camera. You magnificent, magnificent duck."

# EPILOGUE

"I'M TELLING YOU, IT WAS THE BLIND GIRL, THE duck, and the wolf!" yelled Dirk. "They must have jumped off the train."

The police officer sitting across the table from Dirk rolled his eyes and leaned back in his chair. He clicked the pen in his hand three or four times.

"First," said the officer, "stop shouting. Second, enough with the duck story. Just tell me what you were doing with that door open. You realize this is a federal offence, don't you?"

"I don't *realize* anything," insisted Dirk. "That's what happened."

"Right," said the officer. "Look, I just want to fill out this booking sheet and be done with you. Let's try again."

"The blind girl, the duck, and the—"

The officer's chair scraped against the floor as he stood up. "All right, bub. I was just going to write you a ticket, but I think you need to spend a bit of time in lock-up to get your story straight."

The officer led Dirk out of the small office and down a hallway.

"Maybe you should ask some of the other passengers," said Dirk defiantly. "I'm sure someone saw something."

"We did," said the officer, staring straight ahead. "Passengers in your car remember a blind girl with a service dog. No one remembers a duck. And someone said they saw them get off the train in the middle of the night in one of the northern New Brunswick towns. Campbellton or Bathurst."

They walked through a heavy metal door at the end of the hall. The room held half a dozen jail cells facing each other across a narrow walkway. Three of the cells held prisoners.

"Check it out! A new guy!" taunted a bearded man in one of the cells.

"Quiet down, Jones," ordered the officer. "Mr. Bragg is only going to be here until he remembers the reason he was dangling out the open door of a moving train."

The men jeered as the officer pulled a set of keys from his belt.

"I'm telling you, it was the duck, the wolf, and the blind girl!" said Dirk. "Check my camera!"

"Camera?" said the officer, holding the door to an empty cell. "Bragg, we searched the train. We didn't find a camera."

He shoved Dirk into the cell and locked him in. The heavy door to the cellblock closed with a loud *thunk* as the officer left the room.

"I wonder if he'll be a crier," teased one of the prisoners when the guard was finally out of earshot.

"Do you think he misses his mommy?" mocked another.

The other men laughed.

Dirk sat on a bench in his cell. He rested his head in his hands.

"Hey, wait a sec," said the prisoner in the cell across from Dirk's. "I recognize this guy. You're that...what's your name? That guy from the TV."

Dirk looked away.

"Yeaaaaaah, that's you," said the man. "The werewolf guy!"

"I saw that!" said another man.

More laughter rang out from the cells.

"Yeaaaah," said the man opposite Dirk. "That was real funny. What was that song you sang again?"

"I remember, I remember!" said a man with a gravelly voice. "*My wheels belong to the road....*"

The rest of the prisoners joined him for final line of the chorus: "*But my heaaaaaart beloooooooongs to yoooooooooou!*"

All four men laughed and jeered at Dirk. One man rattled his metal drinking cup against his cell bars. Another threw a dirty sock into Dirk's cell.

Dirk closed his eyes and tried to block out the noise. He reached down to tend a sore spot on his ankle that had been bothering him since the train.

"Ow. What the—" he said, pulling up his pant leg. Dried blood stained his skin and sock.

Dirk's mind raced through the last day. The train. The scuffle with the kids. Being dragged by the ankle into the bathroom...by John.

Dirk whistled softly.

"Bit by a werewolf," said Dirk to himself. "That can't be good."